cor sequences...

Consequences

1: Don't Call Me Baby!
2: The Camera Never Lies
3: Runway Girl
4: Secrets, Lies and Videotape
5: Holding the Front Page

Look out for:

6: I'm With the Band

Laurie Depp

consequences...
Holding the front page

Hodder
Children's
Books

A division of Hachette Children's Book

1

Waiting, waiting, waiting. It felt like I was waiting for my life to happen. Waiting to take my A-levels, waiting to leave school and go to uni, waiting to make my own way (without my parents' interference), waiting to discover someone I liked enough to go out with for more than two weeks.

I thought it was all about to start when I found The Story. The one about the runner who pretended he was a TV hotshot and landed up with debts everywhere because he was trying to impress some wannabe model. The Dan Lewis Story. It even got into the paper – the real paper, not just the Sunday women's magazine supplement where I was doing my summer work placement. I thought I was going to explode, I was so ecstatic. An article I'd written (with a little help) was in the national press. Can you believe it? My friend Sally messaged me a photo from the newsagent round the corner from her house. Her finger was pointing to my name on the page: 'By Becky Dunford.'

'Fraudster tells all to our rookie reporter,' the *Courier* had gushed.

And then . . . nothing much changed. After a few days of

everyone congratulating me, it was back pretty much to how it was before. At the *Courier* I was still the work experience girl, sorting out a mess of lipsticks and concealers for the Beauty editor. Had I just blown the beginning of my new life? Had it stalled before it even started?

Of course, I had three more weeks left on a placement that most girls (and some boys) would kill for, and I meant to make the most of them. But why bronze is the new silver and all those stories about people's beautiful homes and how you can look twenty years old when you're actually forty-two . . . they really aren't me. I'm more Orla Guerin than Orla Kiely. (That's the line I've been practising for when I find my perfect boyfriend – although Sally rather spoiled things by pointing out that it will probably be wasted on most straight boys. Orly-who? And whatsa-Keeley?)

I needed to get myself noticed by the news desk – and do it so well that this time they wouldn't forget me again after my fifteen minutes. But how was I going to do that?

My train dragged itself into Swindon station. I wanted it to go faster, hurrying me to London after a weekend in dull, safe Bath.

Don't get me wrong – I love Bath. World Heritage Site and all that. It's beautiful to look at (or most of it is, anyway), with its Georgian terraces and the green hills behind. It's great when you're a kid and want to run around in fields and play hide-and-seek and make dens. But hanging out in the town gets boring as soon as you're past, like, eleven years old. Unless, of course, there's a tourist group to eye up with some cool-looking Italian boys who might take you to a café and talk about film or books or really anything that's Not Rugby. (I can't stand rugby.)

But I wanted more. Or something else. Something faster, and bigger, with more excitement and more possibilities. London. That's what I wanted. London, and to be a proper journalist, and to 'see the world'.

I was on the Monday morning 9.12 – the rush hour was over but there were still some business people on their way to meetings, with their jackets folded neatly beside them. Unusually for the past few weeks, my dad wasn't with me; he's an MP and he had some 'constituency business' this morning. I was sitting by the window, at one of the tables. I was curled up with my iPod and the latest downloads and watching the countryside blur past. In one field a couple of deer were munching grass or leaves; I've seen plenty of deer from the window now that I'm a regular commuter. Across from me a guy in a striped shirt was tapping on his laptop, stopping now and again to answer his mobile. He was loud and glossy and his aftershave was too strong. He had to be an estate agent.

Outside the sun was blazing down, evaporating the early morning rain. Last month, during my exams, had been a heatwave, and another was predicted. But the July weather so far had been wet and disappointing. I'd wanted a steamy summer in London – sunbathing in the park, ice cream melting over my hands (and the hands of someone I might happen to meet?).

Along the carriage was a group about my age. Boys showing off and girls giggling. I could just about see this one boy with dark hair and a sort of I'm-just-into-my-music look, holding himself slightly apart as he listened through his headphones – they were the kind that cover your whole ear.

He wasn't a geeky type. His haircut was too trendy. He looked as though he could be one of those moody and mean characters. I couldn't decide if I disliked him on sight or fancied him. But I couldn't take my eyes off Moody Boy – until his gaze flicked over in my direction and I suddenly became all shy and quickly looked out of the window to pretend that I hadn't been staring. And then slid my eyes back when he turned away again.

Which meant that I missed the beginning of The Conversation.

Because if I hadn't been looking at Moody Boy I'd have taken my earphones out sooner. I really needed to head to the toilets for a pee, but I'd kept putting it off to carry on gawping.

Without my iPod I started to tune in to the chatter around me. In among my thoughts and the need for a pee, a little alarm signal started going off in my head. All I can think is that I'd started to subconsciously pick up on a few key words. The Conversation was coming from the seat directly behind me, so I couldn't see who was talking. But I could hear it was a man: he sounded quite old, but not retirement-home age. He was getting angry with someone, and I could bet it was about something serious. The words 'security', 'unacceptable', 'deal', 'opposition' and 'the goods' zinged into my ears and set off my story radar.

It's amazing how some people can believe that no one else is listening in on their phone calls. Why didn't he lower his voice, or tell the person on the other end that he'd call back later? A train carriage can seem anonymous, filled with so many strangers who don't really matter to your life. But you never know who might be listening.

You never know whether one of them might have an ear for a story that could make her name. And might just happen to have a dictaphone that her darling mother gave her as a gift to mark her going away on work experience.

I'd probably snarled or huffed like an ungrateful brat when Mum gave me the recorder (I know I'm really lucky to have parents who buy me stuff like that, but sometimes I wish they didn't try to plan and provide for everything in my life – especially Mum). It really was a great present though (perhaps I should tell Mum . . .). Tiny and digital, it looked like a silver MP3 player. As I sat on the train I plunged my hand into the depths of my bag to find it among the jumble that's usually in there: creased notebooks, old bits of newspaper, make-up grabbed from the magazine beauty desk, the keys to my dad's London flat . . .

The recorder made a beeping noise as I switched it on and I froze for a second in case The Conversation man had heard. But I wasn't doing anything wrong, was I? So I settled myself back down and tried to stop my heart beating so hard by looking out of the window at the midsummer gold and beige fields.

Eventually, after several centuries, the older man ended his call. I didn't want my dictaphone to beep again, so I left it running. He got up then, and hurried towards the toilet – or perhaps the buffet car. As he dodged past I could see he was wearing a pinstripe suit that looked well cut and expensive (my mother always assesses people by what they're wearing, and I seem to have picked up her habit despite myself – how annoying is that?). I could see that he had grey hair cut short almost to the scalp, to hide where he was starting to go bald, and a pair of square, heavy-framed glasses that dominated his face so much his other features seemed almost invisible. And then he disappeared out of the automatic door and into the no-person's-land between carriages.

What should I do now? What if it hadn't recorded? As casually as I could, I switched off the dictaphone and scrolled through its functions trying to work out how to make it go silent (just in case there was another unmissable call). Ah, that was it: no more beeps from you.

Plugging in the earphones from my iPod, I started to listen. The recording was hard to make out at first, but once I'd got used to it I could hear plenty. I just wasn't sure what it meant. You know when you *know* something's important, but you're not quite sure why? It's all a bit of a puzzle, like when you've seen two people at school who normally hate each other with their heads together, being secretive about something, and at first you can't work out the reason.

Right then the pinstripe suit man strode back. He was frowning, gripping on to his mobile. Maybe he'd realised at last that it wasn't very safe to have a secret conversation when you're between Swindon and Reading and don't know who's listening. I pressed the 'Stop' button on my dictaphone and poised my finger in case I needed to record again. Would he give anything else away?

No. I could hear the rustle and crack of a newspaper, and then quiet. I decided to wait until later to study the rest of the recording. But I found it hard not to keep fiddling with the dictaphone, hoping that I hadn't erased anything.

To divert my attention I made a huge effort and got out my iPod again, and a copy of the *Daily World* that had been scrunched up in my bag. It's the sworn rival of the *Courier*, but, well, you have to read the competition if you want to make an impression in 'the media'. At the *Courier* offices there were heaps of newspapers and magazines everywhere – every title you could think of, pretty much, and enough to fill the recycling boxes of our whole street at home. Alison, who works on the magazine and helped me write the article about Dan Lewis, told me that no one wants to think they're missing out on a hot story that's in the other papers.

Up the carriage, Moody Boy was joining in now with his friends. They were playing a drinking game. There were plastic glasses and cans of Red Bull on the table, and he was pouring vodka chasers.

I'm having trouble even being in the same room as a

bottle of vodka these days. I threw up at a party last month after someone poured a huge chug of vodka into my orange juice and I didn't realise how strong it was. Even the memory of that smell makes me retch. So when Moody Boy catches me gazing over, and holds up a glass with a wink, I'm not interested. And in that moment, with the nauseous memory of vodka vom up close in my nostrils, and something about the wink, I decide I don't like him after all.

Is that mean? He wasn't doing any harm – just drinking a little too early in the day. But no. He'd crossed over, and been crossed off my list. Another one to confess to Sally. She really does despair of me ever managing to go out with anyone ever again. 'So what's wrong with *him?*' she asks, after failure number fifty-three. 'Erm, well, I'm not his type, am I? He likes slinky blondes. And I know he's into rugby. So we don't have anything in common . . .' 'But he's definitely interested, just look at the way he's grinning at you like an idiot – why not give it a go. For once . . .?'

But somehow I just can't manage it. Sally's given up shaking her head at me, or even rolling her eyes skywards. Now she just gives me this long, fake-serious blank look and stabs with her finger: 'Single. Till. You. Die!'

The train was approaching Paddington station. The blazing sun had gone, replaced by more pouring rain. At last we pulled into the platform, under the huge iron arches. Should I try to follow The Conversation man? Sneak along behind him? But then again, I wanted to get into the office as quickly as I could. The deputy editor, Felicity (who's the second-in-command on the magazine, and often comes to tell us what the Editor wants), had said that since I'd already had a story in the paper perhaps I should sit in on the weekly editorial meeting, to see if I had any more scoops where that one came from. So I suppose finding the Dan Lewis Story had done my career chances some good after all.

I reached up to get my backpack off the luggage rack. I tried pulling at it, but it was stuck under something else. The Conversation man stood and effortlessly disentangled it for me. 'Erm, thanks,' I mumbled. It was very weird, having someone you're sort of spying on hand you your case with a smile. And now he was behind me, so I'd have to dawdle around when we got off the train if I was going to follow him.

So I pretended I was having trouble getting my arms through my rucksack (I was, in fact), and for a moment I thought he was going to come and help me with that too. But he dived on past, looking in a big hurry. I tagged along a safe distance behind. He headed for the wide flight of stairs that leads down to the Tube station. I kept track of his cropped head as it bobbed up and down in the sea of commuters and tourists going underground. He touched in with his Oyster card, and I touched in two people behind him. He was going for the Circle and District line, same as me.

On the platform I stood what I reckoned was a reasonable distance away, my eyes flicking between Mr Pinstripe and the indicator board. I needed to change at

Notting Hill, but where was he going? The train took ages to arrive (after three weeks of commuting I wasn't surprised – the Circle line was about the worst for keeping you waiting). I sat down, and he stood. And then I had a decision to make. It was getting late. Would I carry on following him, or make a break for my meeting? I sat pondering, hiding again behind my *Daily World*, reading the same article about fifteen times and still not taking it in. Something about Kate Moss's latest collection at London Fashion Week. I knew I ought to read it properly and try to make an intelligent comment about it in the office, but then it was my stop.

2

Why are magazine supplements called that? Because they're an addition to your newspaper diet – like a vitamin supplement. It's obvious really, but I'd never asked myself before I came along at the end of June to do my six weeks on *Sunday Style*.

Every day I've been coming up to the fourteenth floor of the tower at Canary Wharf – the tower you see on all the aerial views of London, with the pyramid and the blinking light on top. Its official name is 1 Canada Square. They used it as Sir Alan Sugar's office on *The Apprentice* – although he doesn't really work here: his company's head office is in Brentwood, Essex. The newspaper has one floor and we have another, which we share with the Saturday magazine and TV guide and some of the website people – and the canteen.

It's quite cool the way you get here. It's on the Jubilee line, which has all these modern stations that make you feel as though you're in a sci-fi film. At Canary Wharf the roof is a huge arch of glass.

You come out right by what looks like a lake – the whole site is built around and across water that used to be some of the old Thames docks. Once you've followed the stream of office workers off the train and up the escalators that go on forever, you cross the road and climb some steps, then walk through a bright-lit mall with more shops than the whole of Bath.

Then it's through the revolving door – and you emerge into a vast marble atrium. I really did stand there and gasp the first time I saw it. Then someone tripped over my heel and I stumbled forwards to the reception desk. There are so many floors that different lifts go to different sections: floors 1 to 15, 15 to 30, that kind of thing.

And then you have to wait for someone to open the heavy glass doors with their security pass (or at least I do, because I haven't been given a pass of my own). It was Alison, the deputy chief sub-editor, who came to my rescue on the morning of The Conversation.

I'd liked Alison the first time I set eyes on her. She was the only person who lifted her head from what she was doing to really give me a good look and a smile and listen to who I was. With pretty much everybody else I felt as though I was an irrelevance or even an annoyance. It was Alison who explained to me where everyone sat, and what they did, and how the magazine worked.

She told me about her job too. The sub-editors check all the grammar and facts and spelling, she said, and sometimes they have to do quite a lot of rewriting because not all journalists can actually write very well (which was something of a surprise to me).

'So a sub-editor isn't like a deputy editor?' I'd asked Alison, bemusedly, after her explanation.

'No. No, it's quite different,' she'd replied.

Today she was wearing a vintage top and wide jeans. That was something else I liked about her: she had her own style, not just copying what was in the fashion mags or what celebrities had been seen in. The Fashion department wore all their fashiony things – all the latest must-haves – but often thrown together so that they looked a bit of a mess, to be frank.

Not that I can talk. Generally I don't take that much time over what I wear. As long as I've got my favourite jeans and my Converses, then everything's OK. I suppose you might say my style is kind of 'alternative surf girl'. I do like a regular Topshop fix, just like anyone else, but I also order a lot from Howies, which is an ethical 'surfer' brand. Sally and I got into it after our trip to Cornwall last year with the girls' football team. She says that trip is the reason I can't find anyone I like enough to date now. But I'm not sure I'm ready to talk about that yet . . .

'They're just starting,' said Alison, motioning her head over to Jan's office (she's the Editor), where the meeting was taking place. 'Quick, go in.'

The main room had emptied of its senior staff members, leaving behind the 'serfs', as Alison called them: the people who did all the behind-the-scenes work. A cluster of chairs had been moved into Jan's office and everyone was sitting down already. Shit. Should I go in? I slung my rucksack down by the desk I'd been allocated for my stay here and rummaged to get out my pen and notebook. I hated going up and knocking on doors, making an entrance when everyone's head would turn towards me – like going to see the headmistress. But if I was going to become a proper journalist I would have to get used to putting myself in places where I wouldn't always be welcome. After all, I'd managed to go and ring the bell at Dan Lewis's hideout. How much more scary could this be?

I stood by the door, which was ajar, and knocked. Someone had obviously just said something funny, because there was a round of laughter. I poked my head inside. No going back now – I'd been spotted.

'Hello, erm, Becky – are you joining us?' At least Jan-the-Editor remembered my name now; for the first couple of weeks I didn't think she knew I existed.

I nodded, looking around for an empty chair. There wasn't one, so I mumbled and exited again to drag in the nearest swivel office chair. Jan was talking when I came back in, and I was trying not to go all hot and red. I held my head down and tried to be as inconspicuous as possible. Which is difficult when you're dragging a big lump of furniture around with you and knocking into people's feet and bags and having to say sorry about five times.

Two chairs parted to leave a gap for me. On one side was Claire, the Beauty editor. On the other was Nita (what was she doing here?).

Now, you would expect that since the two of us are both

here on work experience, and both the same age, that Nita and I would get on, wouldn't you? (Yeah well, perhaps not, since there are people in my class at school that I've never been able to stand.) But Nita and I are, like, complete opposites. She *loves* all this fashiony stuff and it's her absolute dream to work on a magazine like this. She always looks immaculate – perfectly applied make-up, sleek hair, exactly the right outfit. She seems very self-possessed and the editors are always smiling at her and listening to her ideas. I have to keep reminding myself that it was me who got a story in the paper. Not that I'm competitive or anything.

I had a scribbled list of ideas I wanted to suggest in my dog-eared notebook. I was just waiting for the right moment. I wanted to do some exposés of the world of modelling, and behind the scenes of *Supermodel School*, the TV reality show, and something about whether anti-ageing creams really work, and animal testing, and why don't all cosmetics companies take parabens and other dodgy stuff out of their products. Claire had warned me they might be a bit too 'political' for *Sunday Style* (which is what the magazine's called), but that there was no harm in mentioning them if I got a chance at the meeting.

Claire is tall and wears glasses, and has amazing-looking peachy skin and auburn corkscrew-curl hair. Her family are Irish, from County Kildare, but they moved here when she was quite young. She told me all that when I said how much I liked her accent. She's friendly, but I don't think she has much time to worry about things for me to do. She's always extremely busy talking to PRs and arranging photo-shoots and testing the latest eyeshadow or moisturiser – which is how my mum knows her, because Claire came to the launch of the organic skincare range at the spa where Mum works.

And that's how Mum got to sweet-talk Jan, and how Jan said I could come on this summer work placement. I'd have preferred to be on the main paper, but this is much better than being sat in a local estate agent's office, like Sally, or learning about stock buying (sooo boring) at one of Bath's supermarkets. It's in London, for a start. School even said all us Year Twelve students with placements could skip off after exams so we could start early – they'd prefer that than have us lying around the playing fields making daisy chains and smoking stuff we shouldn't.

At the meeting everyone was ooh-ing and aah-ing over the photo shoot with the latest up-and-coming model star (Zarafina, from Kosovo). She was showing off autumn jackets and boots in the Scottish highlands. I still don't get why the autumn clothes come out in August. The official line is that it's to make people buy all the full-price new season must-haves instead of only snapping up the summer bargains. But surely no one wants to be thinking about it getting cold when they're going on their holidays?

After everyone had sat down again, Nita raised her hand: 'Excuse me, I have some story ideas.'

I frowned. This was supposed to be *my* chance at an editorial meeting . . .

The editors were already smiling and nodding at her. Then she read out four really fluffy, girly stories. She took ages explaining each one.

By the end, Jan had drifted back to examining the notes on her lap with a frown. She glanced up with a brief narrow smile and said, 'Thank you, Nita.' Then she directed her eyes towards the Fashion editor. 'Tallulah, could you work on those with her? I think there are one or two we could use.'

Nita relaxed back on to her seat – was the look on her face smugness or relief?

It was nearly the end of the meeting. Should I dive in now to suggest my obviously more interesting and brilliant ideas? I counted up to ten, the blood thumping in my skull. Was I going to open my mouth or not? Come on . . .

'And how about our star reporter? Becky, do you have anything you'd like to contribute?' Jan asked.

'Erm.' Everyone's heads swivelled towards me and I felt a blush stinging up my neck and cheeks. I really hate blushing; it's so humiliating. But I managed to get three of my ideas out.

'Maybe something on *Supermodel School* would work,' said Jan, brushing her hair away from her face as I finished. Everything she said always seemed to be in a hurry. She wasn't someone who ever looked relaxed. 'We didn't cover it for the start of the series, but it's proved more popular than we were expecting. I'm not sure our advertisers would be too happy about the others, but I see where you're coming from. I'll have a think about them.'

I felt a glow of relief. Then . . .

'Let's get Stephanie to do the *Supermodels*,' Jan added to Emma, the Features editor, who was sitting beside her.

No, no, no! It's my idea, surely I should get to write it? I couldn't believe what I was hearing. One moment, feeling proud that Jan had taken me seriously. The next, everything snatched away.

When I answered the phone to my dad after the meeting I must have sounded really gloomy.

'What's up, Becky?'

'Nothing. Just this silly work placement . . . But you probably wouldn't understand. What are you ringing about?' Dad didn't often call me during the day. He was too busy.

'There's a reception for a new Oxfam report tonight at Westminster that I'm going to. And I wondered if you'd like to come. See what it's all like. What do you think?'

It had been a freakily rollercoaster morning. I said yes, of course. This was exactly the kind of thing I wanted to be doing. There would be serious journalists at the reception, and people involved in charities and development and environmental action. Maybe I'd even see some star reporters, like Kirsty Wark from *Newsnight*.

There was one more thing I had to do before I got my briefing from Claire about my tasks for the day (would I be alphabetising the beauty product samples? Looking up juicy news on the celeb gossip sites? Sorting through the filing cabinets? Only one of those sounded like any fun).

I palmed my dictaphone and breezily announced I was heading for the Ladies. Claire nodded OK. I closed the furthest stall and sat down to listen properly. I still wasn't sure what the man in The Conversation was talking about. Some kind of deal; something that needed to be kept quiet; something that sounded to me as though it was illegal or immoral and would get them into a lot of trouble if someone like me found out exactly what was going on.

3

If you read my blog for 21 July this is what you would have seen:

i'm writing this at midnight cos i'm too excited to sleep yet. 2nite my dad (who's the mp for bath south – there's more about him here) – took me to a big reception at the houses of parliament. it was organised by the charity oxfam – which does all kinds of work on reducing poverty around the world n stuff on climate change too. go visit their site (but remember to come back for the rest of my story afterwards!).

because i'm a bit of a politics-head going to an event like this is something i've always wanted to do – not something i have to be forced into for a school project or anything. i also like spotting mps n especially members of the cabinet. ok i know that sounds totally dorky but cos my dad is an mp it means we talk n think n eat politics 24/7 in our house (when dad's at home that is). it's kind of in my blood! i even write letters to government ministers about issues where i think they're getting it wrong or cud do better!

we took the tube to westminster n i had to struggle not to trip over my shoes on the escalator. i'm so not used to wearing heels that i have to concentrate on what my feet are doing when i wear them (what I didn't realise then is how my shoes were going to totally change my evening!). the station at westminster is like walking on to the set of one of the alien films with lots of concrete arches n vast steel tubes crisscrossing over your head.

as we got to the event i had my head down again, picture-msging my friend sally (this is her <u>profile page</u>). it wasn't exactly the oscars but i didn't want to miss anyone important arriving. i saw grace harlow the new <u>secretary of state for the environment</u> n i heard a whisper that the Prime Minister might even be there!!!

someone i didn't recognise said hello to my father in a loud voice n shook his hand for ages. i was trying to peer past him to spot anyone else from the cabinet. i thought i saw the pm (the Prime Minister) then i thought it couldn't be. but it was – the pm standing right in the same party as me!!

however then a catastrophe occurred that would never happen to my heroines kirsty wark or orla guerin. i misjudged the step into the hall and – crunch! – over went my ankle. dad saved me from splatting on to the floor but it was bad enough. my face went hot n i knew i must be as red as my ruby tuesday nail varnish. that was so not the entrance i wanted. i thought maybe i should just hide behind my hair n slink away right then . . .

but I didn't. i hobbled through n dad introduced me to a load of people who i tried to smile to through the pain in my ankle (though it wasn't as bad as a sprain i got <u>playing football</u>).

<u>rosemarie carlton</u> (she's a new mp for

bristol who my dad has brought to our house a few times) said she was going to look after me. she kept saying i had to do 'rice' n at first i didn't understand what she meant. but then i realised – oh <u>RICE</u>! it's how you treat a sprain: rest, ice, compression, elevation. she made me sit down n felt round my ankle then disappeared n came back with a first aid kit so she cud put on a compression bandage. then she ordered me to stay sitting down for the rest of the evening with my leg up on another chair. how glamorous (not)!

i thought I was going to miss all the fun. in the end i didn't but right then i was gutted n cud feel my eyes going hot n misty . . .

. . . but that's all for now. it's getting really late n i can hardly keep my eyes open so i'll have to finish this 2morrow. come back to find out what becky does next!

4

I woke up in a total grump and couldn't think why. It was raining. Again. Water lashed against the windows of my dad's London flat. My brain was all fuzzy and I couldn't think properly. I was still half in a dream. Ouch! My ankle hurt. I looked at my alarm clock: 6 a.m. It was light, but I felt as though I hadn't slept at all.

I lay in bed and tried to go back to sleep, but it didn't work. I twisted about trying to get comfortable and my head started to throb. Then my mind wandered on to thoughts about the night before and, amazingly, things got significantly better.

Turning my ankle hadn't been such a bad move after all.

I must have been looking really sorry for myself on my chair at the Oxfam launch, foot propped up and ankle bandaged, because Dad kept hovering around and checking on me. He'd dart back between his really important conversations with his really important Oxfam contacts and people from other NGOs (non-governmental organisations, like charities). Emma brought me drinks and snacks and worried over my ankle and whether really I should go home.

24

But whenever she mentioned 'taxi back to the flat' I shook my head so hard and made such a sad, wounded puppy face that in the end she gave up.

Every so often Dad brought people over for me to talk to. Most of them were his cronies – sorry, colleagues – from other South-west constituencies. Anyway, the MP for Exeter or somewhere else down our way would come along, chat for a while, then start to look twitchy at being faced with difficult questions from a teenager (I enjoy asking them hard stuff, like 'What do you really think about nuclear power? I mean if you were given a free vote on it and didn't have to go along with what you're told?'). Then, for some strange reason, they'd mumble an excuse and wander off. Emma's the only one who answers me straight, but we have this agreement (cross-my-heart-and-hope-to-die) that anything she confides in me is 'off the record' and I must Never Tell a Soul.

After about an hour my dad (his name's Tom) came over beaming like the night we won the election, and for a moment I wasn't sure why. And then I saw behind him. Unmistakeable. The PM was loping towards me. In a reflex I looked around to see if he was heading for someone else. But no, it was me he was coming to talk to . . .

'Hello, Becky, how's your foot?' He didn't wait for a response; maybe he had assigned me a time slot and couldn't spend more than a carefully clocked number of minutes (seconds?) on me. 'Tom – your father – tells me you've got a real head for politics. Are you thinking of becoming a researcher for the party? I'm sure you could help your dad out for a start.' He glanced towards my dad.

'Erm, I'd really like to go into journalism, in fact,' I said. 'Be a compaigning reporter for a paper, or the BBC. Thank you.' I'm not sure why I added the 'thank you'; I felt it was polite, because the PM was taking the time to speak to me.

'The other side, eh? Better watch out for this one, Tom! Well, good luck whatever your plans, and I hope your, er, ankle doesn't hold you up too much.'

And then he was gone, whisked away to the next stop on his round of the room.

'Thanks, Dad,' I said, but my father was off to pump hands too.

He gets on much better with this prime minister than the last one. He used to go about slamming doors and moaning 'My career is over!' but he does that far less often now. He's still not sure if he'll get promoted any more and he's pretty resigned he'll never become a minister now. He says he's too old, and all the hungry, ambitious, young MPs are taking over, and overtaking him.

Seeing the PM was the first dramatic and exciting thing to happen that evening. The second was going on behind me.

I had to screw my head around to see. There was a junior minister from the Department for International Development, who I recognised from *Newsnight*, and he was being laid into by another man.

'What's going over there?' I asked Emma, as she brought

me another mango smoothie and some satay prawns on skewers. 'Oh, I don't eat prawns, I'm afraid,' I said when I saw them. 'I always think they look like sea insects. Pink maggots.'

'Maggots? I hadn't thought that way before, but somehow prawns will never look the same again ...' Emma's eyebrows looked as though they would lift off the top of her head. 'That' – she nodded towards the very one-sided argument – 'is Ben Hutchison laying into Mark Bonner. Ooh, he's giving him a right going-over. Poor Mark. Good with the figures and the ideas, not so great at holding firm against a bit of verbal.'

From what I could hear, this Ben was asking every awkward question under the sun. Pouring scorn on the government's failings in the Middle East and Africa, and questioning its commitment. My kind of guy (mentally and politically, I mean). He sounded a bit lashed, but his arguments were sound – some of them the kind of thing my dad berated the Party for behind closed doors.

'So who is Ben Hutchison?'

'He's a journalist,' said Emma, smoothing back a wisp of black hair that had escaped the ponytail grip and the hair wax. 'He's on the *Courier*. Isn't that where your mum sorted out your placement?'

I winced: yes, it was Mum who'd arranged it all; I just didn't like to be reminded I hadn't managed to do it myself. 'Mmm. I definitely haven't seen him though.'

Emma flashed me a grin. 'Yes – there's not many women

would forget seeing Ben Hutchison.'

I think I blushed. It felt as though I had. Don't get me wrong, he *was* cute, in the skinny way that I like, but he looked at least in his mid-twenties . . .

Then suddenly there was a booming voice that didn't fit with the scene: 'Your mum says you're to stay home today and not even think about going to *Sunday Style*. You've to rest that ankle and make sure it mends.'

What? Who was that? The voice was too low to be Emma's.

Oh – Dad. I was lying in the spare bedroom in his flat, and it was Tuesday morning, not Monday night. I must have drifted back into a half-sleep and not heard Dad's knock (he always knocks, unlike Mum).

I made a sulky face. 'But I want to go in today, Dad. Please. There's some things I need to do. And someone I need to see.'

Dad shook his head. 'I have to go to the Commons early for a briefing before the committee starts, but promise me you won't try to go on the Tube or get into work. There's some coffee and some bread for toast. And, er . . .' He was looking out of the door and down the stairs, as though he was checking the contents of the fridge in his head. 'Er, some yogurt too, I think. If your ankle gets really painful, give me a call and we'll see about a doctor.' He frowned. 'Sorry, Becks, I can't be late for this. You'll be OK though, won't you?'

I nodded. ' 'Course, Dad.'

Maybe it wouldn't be so bad staying home. I rang Claire to let her know and she was fine about it. And my ankle did still feel tender. I prodded all round the joint. It was a teeny-tiny bit swollen but not bruised-looking. And I could walk almost without wincing. I reckoned I'd be fine by tomorrow. No doctor was getting near me – you could never tell when they'd suddenly force you to lie down for a week. I did go and fetch some ibuprofen from the bathroom cabinet, though.

I stayed in my PJs until nearly lunchtime (it was still raining; no point going out if I didn't have to), munching my way through morning telly, checking my messages and catching up with friends on Dad's old 'home' laptop, updating my blog and chatting with Sally.

She said her estate agent placement was sooo boring she was nearly asleep all day. The best thing was when she got to go on appointments and nose around other people's houses and see how gross/gorgeous/grimy they were. I told her about the PM and the party, and about The Conversation. She said she wished she was here with me. I wished she was too. Back home we're almost inseparable. People call us 'Sacky' or 'Belly' – like Brangelina, only it doesn't sound so good. If only our parents had given us better names . . .

I made stale-ish peanut butter sandwiches for lunch, because that's about all there was, except for ends of takeaways that Dad hadn't cleared out. And then I ate a tomato and an apple and a piece of celery to try and be healthy.

After that, it was down to business. At least this gave me a chance to really study The Conversation. Apart from a couple of snatched listens I hadn't really had an opportunity to concentrate my full investigative skills on it yet.

I decided to try and transcribe the recording as far as I could. I listened-paused-typed, listened-paused-typed for what seemed like ages. At the end I had one side of a strange conversation that sounded like it was mostly in code, because I didn't know what all the phrases meant. It seemed they were being used in ways they weren't normally. I tried Googling some of them: 'collateral damage', 'Ugandan connection', 'endigeers/endijirs/endejiahs'.

'Collateral damage' I knew anyway. It was used in wars to mean civilians who'd been killed, but I wasn't sure that was what the man in the expensive suit was talking about. If only I could identify who he was, I'd have a much better chance of working out what it all meant.

There was so much about Uganda on the internet that I couldn't tell what this particular 'connection' was. And 'endigeers' came up with nothing except Google prompts asking if I'd misspelled my search. 'Did you mean . . . ?' No I bloody didn't!

It was frustrating.

But, on the other hand, I was becoming more and more certain that I had something. There was one part I kept coming back to. The Conversation man was almost hissing under his breath:

30

'No, no, no. They must not find out. We can't let that happen. OK? Do what you have to . . .'

I played it again. And again. It sent a shiver down my back and arms. Excitement, and the chill of feeling I'd come across something that was dangerous – to somebody or bodies, somewhere.

'We can't let that happen. OK? Do what you have to . . .'

5

It's lucky my ankle was better the next day (or that my dad believed it was), because otherwise I'd have missed some Very Important Events.

Dad's work flat is near the Oval, in Kennington, south of the River Thames. It's not the most glamorous area, apart from the cricket ground (another sport that bores me stupid), which attracts queues of visitors when there are matches on. But I quite like Kennington. I like that it's different from Bath. It's a bit scuzzy and urban. It feels real.

Mum and Dad don't like me walking home here at night. Mum had her bag stolen almost on the doorstep and she gives me a 'taxi allowance' to try and persuade me to use cabs. I like walking at night though. I know I should be careful, and I am – I have this routine where after I've come out of the Tube I look in all directions for anyone suspicious and walk confidently, checking all the way. I stomp along because I've read that then you're less likely to be attacked. When I walk in the dark it feels that all my senses are alive and on alert. I could hear a spider weaving its web or spot the flicker of the slightest movement. It makes my heart race.

It's exhilarating. Night-time is another world from the day.

I've only walked home a few times late enough in the evening for it to be dark. I don't know that many people in London yet. Just Dad, the people at the *Courier*, and my cousins Jake and Isabel, who are both on vacation but supposed to be back soon. I've been out to the cinema a few times, and wandered around Soho and stuff, but mostly I come home, make myself a snack if I haven't had a veggie burger on the way, and chill in front of a DVD or the computer. There are some bands I want to go and see, but to be honest my social life here hasn't exactly taken off. If only Sally was with me we could have a lot of fun. My plan is to stay here for a weekend and work it so Sally can come too.

It was a Wednesday morning, with low, heavy skies. But at least not raining. The pavements were drying, and patterned with piebald patches of dark grey. The morning traffic rushed past me on the main road and the gutter was strewn with leaves that had fallen early. The air was still crisp after the days of rain, but it smelled minerally – of cars and dust and dogshit and something metallic that caught in my throat. It was city air – full of rubbish but full of energy.

I had an Oyster card, which made me feel like a proper Londoner, not just a visitor from the sticks. I trotted down the escalator, past the tiled mural of cricketers (it's the Oval, remember) and the ads for sunglasses and cheap airlines. A warm waft of air came up from the tunnels below. I was catching the Northern line, and then I'd have to change for the Jubilee.

It was rush hour and the platform was full of commuters. There were delays on the line because of signal failure, so the first train was too crowded to get on. Backs, arms and faces were pressed up against the window as people engaged in a real-life game of Twister to try to get themselves to work on time.

A girl next to me had an old Franz Ferdinand track on her iPod. She had red, green and blonde sections through her hair, and wore a short yellow shift dress with pumps. She was carrying a portfolio that she'd customised with paints and stickers. Next to her was a guy in a suit. He was facing away from me. My pulse skipped for a millisecond. But no, it wasn't The Conversation man. Where might he be, among all the millions of faces in the metropolis? What were my chances of bumping into him again? I wondered if he caught the Monday morning train regularly. He'd got on at Bristol, according to his seat reservation (see, I'm good at this, aren't I?), but was that where he lived or where he worked? Or had he been visiting someone there?

When the next Tube train screeched into the station there was nothing for it but to force my way on. Contorted around the pole at the centre of the standing space, I found myself up close to a woman's armpit. Gross.

No one looked particularly happy on the Tube except for a couple of Japanese girls in short skirts and white jackets, laughing together behind their hands. Everyone else had their heads buried in Sudoku. It was a relief to emerge out into the air again at Canary Wharf, and see sky and water –

even though the tall buildings closed in high around you and made you feel small.

I was one of the first to arrive at the offices of *Sunday Style*. Claire and Alison weren't there yet, but of course Nita was sitting at a computer across from me, typing away. She was probably working on one of her article ideas. She looked up at me and half smiled, then dropped her head back down again with a serious face that said to me: 'I'm too important working on my article to be bothered.'

Nita sat unbelievably straight, her nearly-black hair drawn back with an Alice band. She was wearing chunky beads and a neat little bag was perched on the desk next to her. She looked so neat all over. So not like me.

I glanced down at my Converse, ashamed of the ketchup stain on one shoe. I'd rubbed it with some water but that had only made it look worse. Maybe I was a bit scruffy, a bit tangled round the edges. But that's who I am, OK? Just because I was working on a fashion and beauty magazine I shouldn't have to become a slave to all that appearance-obsessed nonsense. Still . . . I frowned over the high-street fashion pages in the current issue of *Sunday Style* and wondered if maybe I should invest in a more girly top like everyone else seemed to wear around here. I could use my untouched taxi money.

When Claire came in she gave me my job for the day: to call back some PRs and research the latest miracle skin serums. A real research job! Not pairing up the Manolos and the Jimmy Choos in the fashion cupboard, or getting rid of last season's press releases. Claire even asked about my ankle and insisted on getting the coffee round so I wouldn't have to put weight on it when I didn't need to. Everyone on the magazine drank endless cappuccinos and cups of tea. The canteen had special trays you could fit the cups into; six cups per tray, like oversized egg cartons.

While Claire was gone Alison came over for a chat, swivelling in Claire's chair. 'How are you? How was the launch party?' I'd told her excitedly on Monday afternoon about my invite.

'Amazing, apart from the ankle of course.' I recounted the highlights of the evening and explained about my blog on the Lifetribe social network. 'Maybe you could join and become one of my "friends" so you can read it,' I whittered. Then wondered if I really wanted someone so adult and cool to see my ramblings. Hopefully Alison would forget about my invitation.

Claire arrived with the coffees and Alison bobbed up off the chair. 'It's Jennifer from the Saturday magazine's birthday today, and we're going out for a drink after work, just somewhere local. Would you like to come?'

'Yeah, cool,' I said.

'Do you need to check with your father or anything? I can talk to him if you like, so he knows you're with someone responsible . . .'

Claire shot a 'What, you? Responsible?' look at Alison. 'I'll be there too,' she said as she handed me my latte. (I've been working my way through the coffee menu here: espresso tastes too bitter, even with sugar; cappuccino is good, but I think latte is my favourite so far, apart from the iced mocha. I bet Ben Hutchison drinks espresso. And smokes.)

'No. Yes. It should be fine.' Dad and I were supposed to be having an 'evening in' with the DVD player for a quality-time father-daughter catch-up. I mean, I like my dad, but this invite sounded, well – more interesting.

I spent the rest of the morning poring over websites and press releases and making PR calls. I felt almost like a real beauty journalist at the end of it. But I wished I'd paid more attention in chemistry and biology class. The PRs kept talking about vitamin C and vitamin E and hydration and nano-everything and collagen and microdermabrasion. I was sure they didn't understand what they were saying any more than I did.

I'm not really fussed what cream I put on my face as long as it's not tested on animals. Not that I ever have to buy anything – Mum always has loads of stuff from the spa lying around the house. It smells OK, and it's free. And it's better for the environment. Mum didn't care about eco anything until, like, about two years ago. Then she discovered that going green was *the* thing to be doing. She started working as financial director for the Midford Vale Eco Spa, and the next thing she was banning us from using plastic bags. But she wears leather shoes, and she doesn't buy ethical clothing, and we eat loads of ready-prepared food because she never has time to cook these days.

'So I've been thinking,' said Claire, after I'd put the

phone down to a woman who was gushingly enthusiastic about 'the future of skincare'. 'We haven't given you many very interesting things to do, have we? I'm sorry about that.' Claire's front teeth had scalloped edges, the kind that are wavy not dead flat. And there was a big gap between them. I read somewhere that Madonna had the space between her teeth closed up, and then decided she wanted it back, so wore braces to have them pulled apart again.

'Anyway,' Claire continued, 'I thought you might like to see a photographer in action. Susie Fay is doing a batch of pack shots for us, and I've arranged for you and Nita to go along this afternoon and take the products to her studio. What do you say?'

'Thank you, that sounds great!' I said. 'We'll be coming back here after, won't we?'

'Yes, if you like. You can get a cab back with the products. No problem. Here's the address you're going to. I've spoken to Nita already, and—'

'Claire! Claire!' It was Tallulah, the Fashion editor, eyes shining, dashing to Claire's side. She linked her arm through Claire's and started trying to pull her towards the glass doors. 'Sorry about this, I'll have her back to you in a sec.' This was addressed to me, with a wink.

'Wait a minute, Tallulah, I'm not finished talking to Becky.' Claire tried to unloop her arm.

'It's important. Please.' Tallulah was bouncing like a very strangely dressed puppy.

'I'm all right,' I said. 'If you need to go.'

'OK . . .' And with that Tallulah whisked Claire outside and started whispering animatedly to her, cupping her hands around Claire's ear. In the time I've been here I've seen Tallulah ecstatically happy and dancing around the room (really – with her shoes off too) because her fashion shoot has come out exactly as she'd like it, and in floods of sobbing tears because it hasn't. Some days she'll grunt at you with a dark look and others she'll be really sweet and bring you coffee and a chocolate biscuit and want to know how you're doing. Talk about moody.

At lunchtime I went to get a sandwich from the canteen. There wasn't time to mooch around the shops or the square because we had to be back in time for the cab. Nita was already eating a sandwich at her desk. Every so often she'd look over. We hadn't discussed that we were going to the photographer's together.

I couldn't decide which sandwich to bag. I stood in front of the chill cabinet, thinking about it and almost deciding, then wandering over to another possibility, putting that down and ambling back in an aimless, fluffy-headed kind of way. Tuna, egg mayonnaise, Cheddar ploughman's, mozzarella and roasted vegetables, hummus and salad. I was picking up the ploughman's (is that your final choice? Yes!) when someone knocked into me and the sandwich slapped on to the floor.

I turned around, still in my sandwich-choice daze, and only slowly realised who had bumped into me. It was Ben Hutchison.

6

Nita and I sat in the back of the cab, a box of beauty products between us. Each looked out of our own window. Each with lips sealed. We had hardly spoken a word the whole journey. She twirled her hair through her fingers. I fiddled with the clasp of my belt.

'Is it right or left here, love?' asked the cab driver. We were at the crossroads with Leonard Street, where Susie Fay had her studio.

'Er, I don't know,' I said. 'We've just got the number. I've never been there.'

'I'll try left then. We can always turn round, eh?'

Along the way we hadn't really needed to talk. Our driver was a proud grandfather: his grandson had recently broken into the first team of a Premiership football club. As he drove and gushed I'd been playing a game with myself. Could I guess who his grandson was before he revealed the name?

Because we were girls – I assumed – he hadn't bothered telling us much in the way of detail; instead he went on and on about how wonderful the boy was and how terrific it was to watch him play. The clues came out in occasional sputters. He was a Spurs player. He was a defender who could also turn his foot to midfield. He'd been picked for the England Under-21 squad.

As the cab pulled up outside the studio (left had been the right way to go after all), Nita laid claim to the beauty box. 'Shall I take this?' she asked.

I nodded. 'OK, yeah.' I wasn't bothered who held the box.

Outside on the kerb the cab driver handed me a clipboard. 'Sign here, please, love.'

I did my scribble. I've been practising a signature, in case I might need one on an occasion like this, aiming for the right combination of sophisticated and mysterious. It came out looking a mess: 'Like an inky spider crawling across the page,' my dad would say, when I was younger and idolised him.

I handed back the board: 'So, your grandson – he's Joey Anderson, isn't he?'

'That's right! I didn't figure you for a fan of the beautiful game. Yes, he's Joey Anderson. You watch out for him next time he's on the telly.' The driver gave me a wink and wheeled the cab around to go back the direction he'd come. 'And a very good day to you.'

'How did you know that?' asked Nita with awe. 'I was nearly dying of boredom in there. I couldn't wait for him to shut up.'

'I play football. I like it,' I said.

Nita smiled shyly. 'Really? I'm useless at sport.' It surprised me to hear Nita admitting she was bad at anything. She always came across as, well – perfect. And, to be honest, a bit intimidating.

I pressed the satiny metal buzzer button on the satiny metal intercom. 'We're from *Sunday Style*. We've brought some things for Susie Fay.'

The air in the street had been thick and warm and dusty. On the other side of the clunky metal door it was cool, with concrete floors and a big industrial lift – one with a huge grille you had to slide across. It made me think of the film I'd seen on DVD – *Factory Girl* – all about Andy Warhol and his Factory studio in 1960s New York. Sienna Miller had played Edie Sedgwick.

We needed the fifth floor. Nita and I had to both haul on the grille to move it. We pulled and shoved to try and drag it into place, Nita hampered by her high heels. It ground across, squealing like an elephant that didn't want to budge. For a while I thought it had beaten us, stubbornly sticking with about fifteen centimetres to go. For a moment I was freaked that we wouldn't be able to get it moving, and we'd be trapped in there with the door wedged too narrowly to squeeze round.

Eventually it clanked shut and, relieved, we dropped against the back wall.

'I thought we weren't going to make that,' I said with a laugh. When the lift reached our floor it creaked open, but much more easily.

'What if we'd been stuck in there? That wouldn't have been fun,' said Nita. 'I don't really like cramped spaces.'

'Me either,' I said, shaking my head.

Susie Fay had spiked blonde hair tied with a silk scarf. She was wearing Capri pants and a stripey, scoop-neck top that was falling off one shoulder. Her eyes were large and brown, the lids weighed down with a paste of black eyeliner.

'Hi, girls. Claire said you were coming along to watch. You're on work experience, right?'

'Yes,' we said in unison.

'Go make yourselves comfortable while I set up. There's some water if you're thirsty.' She motioned over towards a battered leather sofa along one wall of the white studio. Nita and I settled ourselves and looked at copies of *Vogue* and *Harper's* and *Grazia*. Susie Fay was artfully setting up a 'still life with beauty products', adjusting the lights and positions, tilting a huge golden-foiled disc to different angles.

'That's a reflector,' she said, anticipating my question. 'The light's gentler than from the lamps.'

Nita whispered in my ear: 'Who does she remind you of?'

'Did you see *Factory Girl*?' I asked in a hushed voice. Sally and I had raved about the film after we watched it, but I didn't think anyone else was into it like we were.

Nita nodded. 'It's her, Edie, isn't it?'

We smiled at each other and I realised then that Nita wasn't snooty, she was shy. Or maybe a bit snooty, but mainly shy. And she was ambitious, but no more than I was. She was OK.

Susie Fay let us help by moving tubes and boxes and pencils around until they were in exactly the places she wanted them, then clicked some photos and showed us the results on the camera's LCD screen. I was fascinated seeing how Susie worked, and I could see Nita was too.

'Do you want to take some?' Susie asked, after about an hour. We snapped away, taking turns to draw swooshes of lip colour and shave peelings of eyeshadow to make 'creative' effects, or be Mario Testino behind the lens. Some of our photos really weren't bad.

'She was way cool,' I admitted to Nita in the cab back to the office. 'Do you think any other photographer would have let us do all that? Nooo.'

On that journey we hardly paused for breath. By the end I knew that Nita wanted to be a fashion stylist and was going to do A2s in Art, D&T, French and English – as long as her exam results came out OK in August. She lived in north London, in Stamford Hill, and didn't really like her school but was always top of the class. Her parents had paid for her to have a tutor at home. Her grandparents moved to the UK from Uganda, when the dictator Idi Amin threw almost everyone from India out of the country in the 1970s – her family were from Gujarat originally. They'd been granted asylum by the British government. I found out that Nita didn't like much current music. She preferred bands from the 1960s and early 1970s, and maybe some 1980s too, but mostly she liked musicians who were more interesting, different and out there.

'Are you coming to the birthday party?' I asked as we glided up in the lift.

'I wasn't invited, do you think it'll be OK?'

'Why not,' I said, smiling. 'It'll be fun!'

Canary Wharf is surrounded by water. It's part of an archipelago of high-rise islands, gleaming on a sunny day and glowering down when it's grey. You can easily get lost here and, when you do, there's a long way to go to get back where you want to be.

The office party were sitting at the outdoor tables of a champagne bar. Metal-edged café tables-for-two had been pulled together to accommodate the group, and round them was a higgledy-piggledy cluster of wicker-seated, chrome-armed chairs. The tabletops were littered with glasses of beer and lager and wine. No one was drinking WKDs or Ices or Breezers, or anything that wasn't brown or deep red or straw-coloured. No jelly-baby shades for these serious drinkers.

My dad had warned me about journalists and alcohol. Well, not exactly warned, but recounted enough stories about which reporter from which paper had been almost unconscious at which late-night drinking club, or thrown up in the gutter, or drunk the bar tab dry.

Alison was lining up the glasses of white wine and Claire was on red. I call them 'glasses', but they were more the size of mugs. Their wine had been supersized. Tallulah was there with her loyal assistant Marty, and I recognised a

45

couple of the other subs – Andy and David – and Sarah-the-Designer with her head bent in deep conversation with her team. And there were some people from the Features desk who I'd never talked to, plus some others that I guessed must be from other sections of the paper.

Alison had introduced me to the birthday girl, and now Jennifer was asking me what it was like to be the daughter of an MP. I get this so often I've got the answer down ready by now.

'It's not that different from being the daughter of anyone else who works long hours. I mean, if he was a cleaner and worked nights I'd see even less of him.'

'But don't you feel proud that he's making decisions that will affect all of us?'

'Yeah . . . Of course I do. He's really dedicated, and he really cares about his constituents. He's involved in lots of activities and campaigns and initiatives in the community. But it's not so glamorous really, it's just a lot of hard work.'

'A bit like journalism, then!' Alison threw in. 'You did go to that swanky charity party though, didn't you?'

'Yeah . . . It wasn't really . . .' I'd been going to say it wasn't really swanky, because it wasn't fashion-show swanky, or celebrity-opening swanky. But then again, I had been doing my own version of celebrity-spotting there.

Nita was sipping a sparkling mineral water, looking demure and self-contained as normal. David-the-Sub asked her something and she half jumped and then replied with a smile. She said something witty that made him laugh.

'Jennifer says she's going to vote Tory at the next election. Or Green. She can't decide,' said Alison. I think she was just trying to wind us up, because she knows my dad's Labour.

'That's the problem, though, isn't it?' Andy was looming over our table, bright green beer bottle in hand. He leaped into the conversation with both feet. 'No one cares about politics any more. No offence, but they couldn't give a shit whether it's left or right or what. They don't trust the people in power, and don't see how they – themselves – can make a difference. Election turnouts are plummeting, however easy you make it for people to vote. And the younger generation . . .' (Andy was thirty something) '. . . there's nothing for them to connect with. No one to admire. Politicians are useless fucks, the whole lot of them.'

Andy had downed a few Becks. He was usually quiet in the office.

'I don't think I agree with that,' I said, softly but sharply. My face was flushing. I wasn't sure if it was anger or embarrassment. I felt as though I had to defend my dad, because I know he's a good person, good at his job.

'Labour's deserted the working class and that's what's let fascist bastards like the BNP get a foothold . . .' Andy continued.

Alison had poured some of her wine into a glass with ice for me. The stem was cold; the bowl was beaded with condensation, like a pattern of pebbles. I could see that she was muttering at Andy with annoyance and drawing him away. The legs of his chair screeched across the paving stones. 'No sensitivity ... typical bloke ... she's only seventeen,' came wafting to me through the evening air.

Then, from up above, someone said in a clear voice, 'I care. And they're not all useless fucks. Just some of them. Am I too old to count as the younger generation?'

It was my third encounter in two days with Ben Hutchison. Surely this couldn't be coincidence. I don't get all that Cosmic Ordering rubbish (I found a book about it when I was looking under Mum and Dad's bed for a hairdryer because mine had broken down), but maybe the universe was trying to tell me something.

7

My blog for Thursday 24 July:

after my amazing evening last night
absolutely nothing happened today. nita n
i were first in the office again (apart
from poppy who's jan's personal assistant).
everyone else rolled in after 10am holding
their heads and complaining about feeling
ill and tired. the only other person who
wasn't suffering was jan-the-editor but
then she didn't come to jennifer's birthday
drink. alison said that's why everyone was
being so loud n getting lashed – because
'when the cat's away the mice will play'.
i think i got what she meant . . .

today is dad's last one in parliament
before the summer recess. it means he'll
be qoinq back to bath at the weekend n so
i'll be ordered to take the train back with

him. which means another weekend i'm not allowed to be in london on my own (boohoo) - tho of course it'll be lovely to see you sally!!;)

after dad catches up with some stuff for his bath south constituency he n mum are going to scotland on hols. my problem is how do i persuade them to let me stay here in london on my own in dad's flat while they're hundreds of miles away? (post me your ideas!)

you might be wondering why i haven't yet revealed what happened after dashing sir hutchison came to my rescue on his white charger (or is that 'warm lager'?). well that's because i wanted to build up the anticipation. not give you the story too quickly but space it out so you really really want to know what i'm going to tell you (and no comments filled with zzzzzzzzzs or boringboringboring thank you!). we had an after-school workshop in the spring term with a guest speaker who's a film lecturer n he showed us how films deliberately reveal their stories bit by bit. this film called memento - where the story is told in reverse - was especially clever. <u>guy pearce</u> (the director n he starred in it) is my hero. i wrote about memento n the <u>film lecturer visit</u> in february.

i don't think i can quite manage to tell my story in reverse so i'm going to stick with the right way round!

so after ben 'rescued' me he came over n sat at our table. he has a yorkshire accent and lovely eyes but when i picture him for some reason i can't remember if they r green or grey - it's like they keep changing in my head. but his hair is definitely brown - lightish not dark.

he's very funny n sharp n bright. he was talking with alison at first n her eyes were all sparkly as they were pretend-arguing. n then suddenly ben was talking to me! he said he'd read my story about dan lewis the runaway runner n had been wanting to ask me about it (a real journalist wanting to ask me about a story!) n tell me how he thought it was really well written n it showed great initiative that i'd tracked dan lewis down on my own. ben said he thought i had a good nose for a story n cud have a future in journalism!!

he was really interested in what i had to say. i told him all about my dad and how he's on the environmental audit committee n how i want to be a proper journalist n that i'd seen him at the oxfam launch laying into mark bonner. tho he looked a bit embarrassed about that.

we were talking for ages. i didn't realise what time it was till nita said she was going home. it was after 11! my mobile said dad had tried to call five times. ben found cabs for me n nita which was really nice of him n i rang dad from the car. he wasn't too pleased at first but he was ok when i got back. except he was looking quite tired n stressed i don't know what about.

but the best bit is that ben said i can help him out with the story he's working on! tho when I went down to find his desk today the woman who sits next to him told me he was out of the office. which was

disappointing. but i'm sure he meant it
don't you think? it wud be mean to just say
that n get my hopes up.

8

When I went to visit Dan Lewis, after I'd tracked down the infamous high-spending runaway runner to a small council flat, I think he thought I was a proper journalist, and older (I put on more make-up than usual and borrowed some of Mum's clothes that she keeps in Dad's flat). I had to improvise when he tried to shut the door on me. But I'd gone canvassing for the Party at the last elections, and Sally and I used to compete with each other to see who could keep the door open longest with a voter who really didn't want us there. So he didn't stand a chance of keeping me out.

I had to improvise too because I didn't have any business cards. Instead I gave him a copy of the magazine with my name written on it. I was quite pleased with my quick thinking, but he was so snarly with me and world-weary-looking that I never thought he'd call. And he didn't – but he sent me something even better: the tape telling me everything.

It was Jake – my cousin – who'd put me on to the Dan Lewis Story. He emailed me the link to the film Dan had made about everything he and all the others had got up to at his production company. Jake said he recognised him. Only the boy he knew was called Bryan. They went to the same college, when Jake and his family were living in Suburbia, and they were both studying film and video. They worked on a project together one time, and Bryan (aka Dan) gave Jake his number. Did I want it? And by the way, Jake knew which company it must be that Bryan/Dan had been working for. He had a number there too . . .

I've always had this great email relationship with Jake. He's like my second big brother. In fact, if I'm really honest, I get on better with Jake than with my real big bro, Matt. But perhaps that's because I've never had to put up with his inane, rugby-loving, smelly, straight, boring friends. And he's never cut up my favourite bunny soft toy from when I was three. I still haven't forgiven Matt for that. (I got my own back with his Action Man, though.) Jake's not into politics or almost any of my other obsessions (war correspondents, boys with sharp cheekbones, making poverty history, Team Bath FC). He's one of those arty types and likes all this really cool music. He's always giving me tips for bands. Now he's studying at the London College of Communication and renting a room in Camden and hanging around with all these 'in' people.

I'd been wailing and moaning on to Jake about my *Sunday Style* placement, and how I really sooo wanted to be doing proper journalism instead, and he said he'd let me know if he had any ideas. At first I thought he was going to get me some gossip or an interview with one of the bands he knows.

But he came up with Dan Lewis, and that's good enough for me.

Now I was about to be working with a real news journalist on a national paper. (Last I heard, my story hadn't done the runaway runner any harm either – it had helped get his name noticed too, and Dan Lewis was about to begin filming on a documentary for the BBC.)

You wouldn't particularly have noticed Ben Hutchison's desk among all the other desks in the open-plan office, except for the Bradford City clippings taped to the side of his monitor. The desk was grey, and arranged over it, in no particular order, were a grimy computer, a phone, a stack of filing trays and heaps of papers. Pens were strewn about, and the surface was marked with coffee cup rings (they looked like espresso to me). A grey office chair with plastic foam showing through the frayed seat material was pulled out from the desk at an angle, as though someone had evacuated it at great speed.

'I'm sure he'll be back soon. He's probably just gone to get some lunch,' said the same woman I'd seen yesterday, smiling sweetly. I wasn't in a mood for sweet smiles. I'd just had a ruck with my mum on the phone, and only the thought of working with Ben was keeping me from full-blown grumpiness.

'Given in to his nicotine addiction at last and gone out for a quick cigarette, more likely,' mumbled a head bent right over a keyboard. The head snapped up straight. 'I've got an hour to finish this and it's all wrong. I can't get hold of any of the people I need to speak to . . .' The head frowned deeply. 'Damn.'

Ben appeared at the glass doors into the office, using one hand to touch his security card to the sensor and the other to grasp on to a fistful of sandwiches, crisps and chocolate bars.

'Have you had lunch?' he asked as he walked up. 'I got you this . . .' It was a ham and salad sandwich. I don't eat ham.

'Thanks. Erm, I've had something already.'

I was lying – in fact I was starving – but I didn't want to seem ungrateful.

'You can sit over there, opposite me. Richard's away – don't mind his stuff, just shove it in a drawer if you need more space. How much time d'you have?'

I checked on my mobile. 'I'm supposed to be back in half an hour.' I was moonlighting in my lunch hour, sneaking down to the big, bad underworld of the newspaper, away from the shiny, bright lands of *Sunday Style*. I felt like I did when Sally and I bunked off school a couple of times. (Only twice, ever – I'm such a good girl, aren't I? But the sad truth is I actually enjoy school. Or most of it.)

Nervously, I edged some papers into a sort of pile towards the edge of Richard's desk. I switched on his computer and eyed the phone. It had more buttons and more unintelligible symbols than the one I was using upstairs. The lead between the base and handset was wound into a rope of knots.

'To go with my story I need to get some quotes from junior doctors at different hospitals, and medical students who are looking for training places. Here's the number of the BMA – that's the British Medical Association – and here are some others that you can try.' Ben handed me a sheaf of Post-It notes with scrawled numbers. His handwriting was hard to make out; even worse than mine. 'See who you can track down and what they think of the training they're getting, or if the students about to qualify are planning on heading abroad. OK?'

Ben munched on his sandwich and started tapping at his keyboard. Occasionally he'd share a joke with the woman next to him. I wondered if I should try to join in . . . But even if I could think of something witty to say, quickly enough, I wasn't sure he'd notice. I could see the top of his head above the monitor but to talk to him I'd have to crane around the computers or stand up. I decided instead to show him how committed and professional I was by getting on with the job he'd given me and not making a fuss. Luckily my time on *Sunday Style* had got me used to ringing up people who didn't know who on earth I was.

Years ago my dad used to be a Parliamentary Under Secretary of State in the Department of Health (it was a junior ministerial role but still pretty important). I knew a little about this story already, because he still followed the health news. Ben had emailed me an outline of what he was writing. It was about a medical 'brain drain' – doctors heading abroad because they couldn't get the training they wanted in the UK.

In my half-hour I made a lot of phone calls but only got

one actual quote. Leaving a message with my name and mobile number and who I was working for became a practised patter.

Back upstairs that afternoon I kept having to duck into corners or pretend to need the loo, or go and get yet more coffees and snacks, so I could answer all the calls that started coming in. Claire was giving me funny looks. 'Can I ask what you're up to there, Becky?' She said it nicely, not like a teacher in class, but even so I froze and stammered.

'It's, well, it's, it's, ah, um . . .'

'It's all right, you don't have to tell me. Just try not to make it too obvious, OK?'

I met Alison in the toilets and told her what was going on.

'Working with Ben Hutchison, are you?' she said as she dried her hands on the roller-towel. I wasn't sure if she was happy for me or envious.

Nita knew what I was doing as well. Since two days ago we'd been messaging each other through Lifetribe all the time. Sally couldn't get online at her estate agent – she didn't even have a desk of her own to sit at – so I had to wait until the evenings to catch up with her. Usually I'd call at lunchtime, but today I hadn't managed to, because of my assignment with Ben.

I was supposed to be helping Stephanie with a fact box charting the highlights of *Supermodel School* – my idea – but I couldn't concentrate. I kept cyber-wandering – looking up articles that Ben had written (everything from telephone call-in quiz scandals to the possibility of nuclear power stations being flooded if sea levels rose, plus some obituaries and music reviews). And then there were my junior doctors calling back. At last I had enough quotes to email Ben.

'Thanks!' he emailed back. 'You're a star. Fancy doing some more next week?'

I was tired but happy by the end of the day. My ankle had decided that maybe it wasn't completely all right. It was throbbing. But I didn't care.

I gazed out of the floor-to-ceiling windows next to Jan's office. The view was spectacular. London spread out like on Google Earth, all shades of grey and glinting in the sunlight. It was hazy down below us, a pall of fumes softening the edges of the buildings. I could see St Paul's cathedral and the 'Gherkin' and, out in the distance, the London Eye.

'Time to go, Becky.' Claire woke me from my dream. 'You really haven't been with us this afternoon, have you?'

'Sorry. It's Friday – I'm finding it hard to, you know, focus.' I checked the computer clock. 'I better had go,' I said, scrambling under my desk for my backpack. 'I need to meet Dad at Paddington for our train.'

I rushed out through the doors with only time to wave a goodbye to Alison and Nita. I was sure I must have forgotten something. Backpack, iPod, bag, magazine, today's *Courier* . . . No, maybe I was all right.

On the DLR I realised what it was. I'd left my reporter's notebook on the desk I was using. I texted Nita. She was still in the office. `all ok :)` she texted back. `safe in my bag. c u mon. nx`

We were catching the 6.01 train, so we'd be in Bath by half-past seven. Mum wanted us home in time for dinner, because Matt had announced he was going to be back from uni. She'd tried telling me at lunchtime to leave my work placement early in the afternoon, but I'd explained that I needed to stay – it wouldn't look good to keep taking time off, and I'd already missed Tuesday because of my ankle. Neither of us wanted to give in, so we ended up having one of our arguments and I hung up on her.

When I came up into Paddington station from the Tube I saw that Dad had texted saying he was running late, so I should go and find our seats.

I was getting worried he wouldn't make it, but he arrived just as the train was beginning to lurch out of the station. He squeezed down the aisle and shot his briefcase up on to the overhead shelf, after taking out a manila file.

'Sorry, Becky, I got caught up in something. You all right?'

I nodded.

'How was your day?' he asked as he manoeuvred himself into the seat opposite me across the table. I had the one facing forwards.

'Pretty good,' I replied. 'I'm helping a journalist on the paper with a story about junior doctors.' I hadn't told Dad before about Ben. Not even during our rescheduled pizza-and-DVD session the evening before.

'That sounds more interesting than face creams,' he said, and we shared a grin. Dad understands my limited interest in beauty products. 'But mind you don't upset the editor on the magazine by neglecting what you're doing there.'

'I know, Dad – don't piss people off unless you really have to.'

'Language, Becky!' Dad was only half serious, and mainly because we were in public. As long as I don't use anything too strong he's pretty cool about a bit of swearing here and there. He says it's his 'cunning strategy': don't make swearing taboo, and then it's not so exciting to do it.

He looked drained, but then he always does by the end of a Parliamentary Session. He hadn't shaved and his hair needed cutting. Dad's hair is almost completely grey, but at least he's not going bald. He was wearing jeans and a green polo shirt instead of a worky suit (he'd 'broken up' for his summer hols, of course).

As dads go, I think he's one of the better ones. He's mainly been a 'weekend dad' because of needing to come up to Westminster for Parliament during the week. And then often he'll only have half a weekend because he needs to do his constituency surgeries – where he looks into problems that the people or Bath South bring to him, and issues in the region. Then he has to make various 'appearances' locally, visiting the over-60s group in Timsbury, or opening a fête in Freshford. But when he is around he's always had lots of time for me and Matt – reading stories and taking us out when we were young; coming to football matches (mine) and rugby games (Matt's) as we got older. He doesn't treat us like children; he'll have a proper debate with us if we disagree with him.

Mum's always been around more, but our relationship is trickier, and liable to occasional explosions when one or the other of us doesn't get our way. Matt adores Mum and always gives me a hard time when I get on her case. But I can't help it – she always seems to want me to be different from how I am, and fit in with her plans for my life. Matt says we're a combustible mix because we're too similar – although I can't see it.

Before Matt and I started school Mum stayed at home to look after us, then she took on some part-time work – book-keeping and accounts – and the au pairs began to arrive. We had three of them altogether. I remember Sonia best. She was Polish and used to braid my hair and comb and pin it into different styles. We'd dress up together in Mum's clothes and jewellery, but Mum never guessed. At least, I don't think she did.

On the train, I was listening to my iPod and daydreaming about how The Conversation would be a huge exposé, and I'd become a star reporter on the *Courier*, and travel the world after uni, uncovering injustices and doing reports for *Newsnight*. And then maybe I'd write a book about everything and Ben Hutchison would be at the book party . . .

Dad was reading the contents of his manila file. I've always liked that word: 'manila'. When I was a kid I thought it was something to do with vanilla – that maybe the folders tasted of ice cream. I looked it up on Wikipedia a while ago. The name comes from the stuff the files were originally made from – something called manila hemp. It's related to the banana and comes from the Philippines, whose capital is Manila . . .

I wondered if Alison fancied Ben.

9

Everything in London was so fast. And everything in Bath was so slow. People walked more slowly, talked more slowly. Visitors to the city ambled along, marvelling at the architecture, and residents got on with their weekend shopping. You could see a world of people in London. Bath was one-dimensional by comparison. The vast majority of faces were white and apart from the tourists and the Polish bus drivers they nearly all spoke English as their first language. I hadn't properly noticed that, before this summer.

Things had been moving quickly for me, too. And now I wanted to be back in the frantic, smelly world of the capital. I mean, it was nice to see Matt again, and great to meet up with Sally – we had a brilliant time hanging out and going to the shops and then out in the evening to a party that someone in our class was having because their parents were away. But I felt weird being home again. Somehow out of step with everyone. When I wrote about this weekend in my blog it was as though I was pretending to be someone else. Me-before-London.

It wasn't as though much had happened in the few weeks I'd spent there. But enough to give me a scent of a life that was different from the one I had in Bath. I even felt a distance between me and Sally. Only very slight; a tiny gap of wistfulness. I was planning to talk to her about it, but then I didn't want to bring her down, so I just kept to the exciting bits about the magazine shoot and Ben Hutchison. (She thinks I fancy him.)

Sally was happy because it looked as though she was finally getting together with Steve, who she'd been eyeing up all year. He did have a girlfriend but they'd just split up, and he admitted at the party that he'd really liked Sally for a long time.

I had a snog with someone too, but I'm not even going to tell you his name because he was such a bad kisser and, again, really not my type. It was just that kind of time in the evening. The sun was setting over the hills, and Sally was wrapped around Steve, and I'd drunk about the right amount, and it happened. Dad insisted on coming to pick me up and for once I didn't try to stop him.

All over the weekend Mum and Dad seemed grouchy with each other. Matt shrugged his shoulders when I asked if he knew what it was about. After the relative quiet in our house lately I hoped they weren't going to kick off and start the weekly rows again. As soon as I heard raised voices I shut the door to my room.

I'd emailed The Conversation to myself and on Sunday I read and re-read it on my computer. I used to share the old 'family' computer with Matt, but he managed to persuade Mum to buy him a new one as a going-to-university present. So now the old one sat among the mess on my homework table.

I wondered what I should do with the transcript I'd made . . . Without knowing who the pinstripe suit man was, I didn't think I could find out a great deal more myself. And I didn't want to post it online and ask for help there because I felt it was *my* story – and it was supposed to be my ticket to journalistic fame.

As far as I could see, I had four options.

One – forget about the whole thing. After being so excited at first, The Conversation had slipped into the background in the whirlwind that was the end of last week. Sometimes I wondered if I really had heard something important – or if my overactive imagination was deluding me (my mother's always saying that's my trouble).

Two – ask my dad if he had any ideas. He knows loads of people, and there was a slim chance he might recognise either Mr Pinstripe or else some of the things I'd heard. On the other hand, he might not. Or he might tell me not to get involved. Or that I was being stupid. (I don't particularly want to feel stupid in front of my dad.)

Three – without giving away why I wanted to find out about them, I could ask online about some of the terms I'd Googled. This was fairly low risk. I could do it through political chat rooms and activist and NGO sites and forums (I was convinced politics was involved here somewhere). But there was a large chance it wouldn't give me anything more than Google had.

Four – take it to Ben Hutchison and see if he could help me uncover the story. In terms of personal credibility, this was the highest risk. It could mean me looking really sad and silly and deranged in front of Ben. I could just imagine him now, joking about it with the woman who sat next to him.

Which would it be?

I fluttered over the options in my mind and pulled open the doors of my wardrobe. I peered into drawers and under my bed. What should I take for my next week in London? With dad back in Bath I'd be there on my own most of the time, which I was really looking forward to: proper freedom. Jake was back now from his holidays and my parents had agreed he would 'chaperone' me to check I didn't get up to anything dodgy. But if he'd emailed them what he'd emailed me I bet they wouldn't be trusting their little girl to his care – Mum and Dad probably think he's still like he was when he was eight years old and cute.

All my clothes looked boring. There were too many plain colours and things I wasn't sure really suited me. I felt frumpy and dull and not at all fit for London. I stared into the mirror on my white chest of drawers and tested out different model-like expressions. But I looked ridiculous. Perhaps I should try something new with my hair, like Edie-style platinum blonde.

I knew I could never look like one of the models in *Vogue* – or even *Sunday Style*. I'd seen how they were all digitally

68

enhanced to appear superhumanly perfect, but knowing it was a fake didn't stop me feeling my own looks were somehow inferior. My skin was too patchy and it was prone to more than the odd spot now and then. My make-up, when I wore it, was sooo last year, and I couldn't put it on properly anyway. My shoulders were too wide and my breasts too small and my eyes were the wrong colour. I stuck my face close to the glass and studied every single pore of my nose. I knew I should resist pressing the blackheads, but they're so tempting . . . A while ago I got into using those pore tapes to pull them out, until I read online about how they can damage your skin, and you might just as well use Sellotape.

In the end I gave up on my inspection. It was making me feel bad. Perhaps I should stop reading those fashion magazines. I was sure Orla Guerin wasn't so self-obsessed. She wouldn't worry about a few blackheads. Would she?

10

'I've, er, well . . . I was wondering if you'd have a look at something I've been working on. I mean, I'm sure it's nothing, but it may be something. In fact, I think it may be something important, and perhaps illegal. It might be some kind of scandal. But I'm not sure, so I wondered . . .'

I wasn't being my most articulate. Still, you have to give me points for having the bottle to take The Conversation to Ben and get the sentence out at all.

He was smiling, patiently – a kind of 'What on earth is she talking about?' smile, and then relief at the end when I'd just about made sense. 'Yeah. Yeah, I'll take a look. D'you want to email it to me? Is it urgent?'

I'd decided to go straight to Ben's desk as soon as I got to the office: not give myself any time to have cold feet and convince myself it wasn't worth it.

'I'm not sure if it's urgent. But it might be. Thanks. It'd be great if you could let me know what you think. Shall I come by at lunchtime?'

'Yeah. Come along then and we can look at it together,' Ben replied.

Something in my chest leaped at the word 'together'. Ben opened the door for me and I took the lift up to the *Sunday Style* floor.

I've found out that Ben is twenty-six. I don't think he's going out with anyone, but I got Nita to ask Tallulah's assistant, Marty, because if anything's going on in the office he's the one who'll know.

' "Ben, oh yes, Ben . . ." ' Nita almost exactly mimicked Marty's lilting voice as we shared sandwiches and crisps in the grassy square outside the office. ' "He's one of my favourites on the paper. Cute Yorkshire accent . . . Nice eyes . . . I heard he split up with someone a few months ago – and he's been heartbroken ever since, poor boy. Or at least not dating anyone properly' – or I think that's what Marty said. So I'm not sure if that means he's not interested, or sleeping around. Could be either . . .' Nita took a large bite of prawn sandwich.

'Thanks, I think,' I said, flatly. 'That's not exactly what I wanted to hear.' We were taking an early lunch so I could go and do my 'moonlighting' on a full stomach this time. Neither of us had been invited to the editorial meeting this week, so we'd been able to nip off without anyone noticing.

'But you're not supposed to be after him, are you?' Nita teased. 'I thought you were only interested in his mind and journalistic potential.'

I threw a crisp at her. Nita caught it and ate it. 'So? Do you like him or what?'

'I don't know,' I said. And I was being truthful. 'I mean, like, he's nine whole years older than me. Seven years older than Matt and Jake. When he was my age I was . . . er . . .'

'Eight,' said Nita.

'Right, eight . . . So he won't even notice me in that way, will he? And anyway, being so ancient he probably has really awful taste in music and films and we'd have nothing to talk about . . .'

'Except news and politics – two of your favourite subjects,' Nita pointed out, unhelpfully.

My heart kept doing annoying little jumps whenever a thought involving Ben popped into my head. I didn't want to fancy someone where it would be so complicated even if anything happened (which, of course, it wouldn't). Why couldn't I go for a boy where it would be easy, and right, and he wouldn't turn out to already have a girlfriend, or be from a completely different generation?

I munched on my crisps and stared down at blades of grass and white daisies. I wasn't sure I could bear thinking about all this any more right now, so I waited long enough for Nita to change the subject.

'Anyway, Tallulah's given me tickets to a shop-opening this evening,' she said. 'It's a friend of hers. If we like anything we'll be able to get a discount. Interested? It could be a laugh. And you were saying you wanted some new clothes.'

'Maybe,' I said, getting up and dusting off my jeans. 'I'll let you know. Need to go now. I'll see you later. Upstairs.'

I moved off quickly so Nita wouldn't follow me. 'Bye,' I said over my shoulder.

'Bye then,' I heard from the grass behind me.

Perhaps wolfing down a sandwich hadn't been such a clever idea. My stomach was knotting up and I felt a little giddy from the sunshine. The weather was starting to turn hotter, as the forecasts had predicted.

I dragged my feet through the marble atrium of 1 Canada Square and up in the lift, counting off the floors on the display. I was excited and apprehensive. What if I'd made a complete fool of myself? What if The Conversation really was nothing? I'd survive it, of course – like missing an open goal, or, even worse, scoring an own goal. But it wouldn't be pleasant. And what if it meant Ben didn't trust me any more and wouldn't let me help with his other stories?

Ben was at his desk, frowning and typing. He was hunched over, squinting at the screen. I wondered if he needed glasses. Mum looks like that at the computer when she doesn't wear hers.

'It's your little helper to see you, Ben,' said one of the other journalists, with a smirk, when Ben didn't notice me walking up to his desk. I blushed and felt annoyed at the same time. It was so patronising talking about me like that – as though I wasn't there, or didn't count.

'Mm? Oh! Hi, Becky.' Ben gave the man a withering look.

'Hi, Ben,' I said, coughing, my throat dry with nerves.

'You OK? Want some water?' Ben took the bottle that

was on his desk and offered it to me. I took a swig.

'Fine now, thanks,' I said, my eyes watering from the not-quite-coughing-fit.

'Look, I'm sorry, Becky, I'm on deadline and I'm really pushed, right? I have to get this over to the subs for three o'clock. And I'm not sure there's anything you can do to help with it . . .'

Perhaps he saw my look of disappointment, or perhaps he was going to say the next words anyway . . .

'But there was something you wanted me to look at, wasn't there? Just let me finish this paragraph, and I'll be with you – I can only spare about five minutes though.'

'OK.'

I stood, silent, and looked around. Rows of desks and filing cabinets reached off into the distance. At first I didn't have a clue what they all had to do with producing a newspaper. But as I watched, some of the picture started to make sense. People were walking around with large paper sheets, printed with pages from tomorrow's newspaper. The printouts were being spewed by a set of computer printers lined up on some tables at the end of the office. One guy was standing at a photocopier, making more large copies of the pages.

'Richard's still away,' announced the woman who sat next to Ben. 'You can sit at his desk again.'

I edged over and perched on the chair, placing my purse on the desk. I hoped Ben wouldn't be long; this waiting was excruciating.

A copy of that day's paper was lying on the floor. I picked it up and flicked through. There was Ben's junior doctor story. They'd used some of my quotes, but my name wasn't on the piece anywhere. I hadn't really expected it to be, but I couldn't help being a teeny bit disappointed.

And then a dark-haired woman came up to Ben: 'I've got the images for your piece. Can you come over and take a look? Only the designers want to get started with a rough layout.'

That would mean more waiting.

Ben jumped out of his chair, leaving it spinning. Off he strode, across the room. I could hear him chatting and joking with the woman.

Ben's desk neighbour gave me a smile. 'It's Becky, isn't it? Ben hasn't introduced us – which is very rude of him. I'm Sarah.'

'Hello,' I said, and leaned over to shake the hand she was reaching across the mountain range of computers.

'I hear your dad's an MP – is that right?'

'Yes.'

'What's his name? I've probably been at some kind of Parliamentary briefing with him.'

'Tom Dunford. Bath South.'

My answers were short because I was feeling nervous. I wasn't paying proper attention to what Sarah was saying. She was trying to be friendly. But I wasn't really interested.

'Oh, Tom Dunford . . . I thought you had a West Country accent, or Bristol or somewhere round there. He was tipped for great things before all the reshuffles pre the last election, wasn't he? What's he up to now?'

'Environmental Audit Committee.'

'Oh right.'

I knew it sounded like a comedown, after Dad's previous position. He wasn't even chairing the committee.

There was a pause, and then Sarah said brightly, 'So have you been feeding Ben some juicy Westminster gossip? He's always keen to make new contacts . . .'

Across the office, a figure with mid-brown hair and a blue shirt was weaving his way between the desks, getting larger as he approached. I felt a sense of relief. Ben was coming back.

'Sorry 'bout that, Becky,' he said. 'I promise I'll give you those five minutes – right here, right now. Let's find your email . . .'

Ben scrolled down his inbox. My email was unopened. I tried not to feel disappointed – it had taken me ages to write, while I was supposed to be sorting out Claire's post. I'd kept the message professional-but-friendly. I'd written 'Becky' instead of 'Becks' or 'B' at the end and I certainly hadn't put any xxxs.

Ben opened the attachment. I drew up a chair that no one was using so I could sit next to him.

Ben read. After a while he turned to me: 'This looks really interesting. I think you may have something here. Sounds like somebody's up to something naughty that they don't want found out . . .' At last I could breathe again. I hadn't made a total tit of myself! 'But I'm not sure how much further we can get if we don't know who's speaking. That's the key, isn't it?'

'Yes.' Reluctantly, I agreed. 'But the problem is I didn't recognise him. He could be anyone.'

'What did he look like?'

I described the man in the pinstripe suit.

Ben shook his head and gnawed at his thumb as he concentrated. 'It's too difficult to tell. Doesn't bring up anyone I know, from what you've said. I don't suppose you took a photo – you know, with your phone?'

'Sorry, no. I didn't think.' I'd felt so pleased with myself for recording The Conversation, and now I realised I should have snapped Mr Pinstripe to get an ID. Stupid. I could have done it while he was walking along the platform – pretended to be a tourist awestruck by the glories of Paddington station's iron and glass arches. *Click*. He wouldn't have known that in fact he was the star of my photo.

'Never mind,' said Ben. 'So that angle's no go . . .' He was thinking aloud. 'What about the original recording? I doubt I'll get any more from it than you, but what if I have a listen?'

'I've got it upstairs, in my bag,' I said.

He looked at his watch. 'Shit. I've got to get back to my story. How about we get out of here for coffee after I've finished? I'll text you. What's your number again?'

He wrote it down on his hand. Black biro on his tanned skin.

'See you later . . .' And with that, he turned back to his article and began to frown and hunch again.

Now all I had to do was think up an excuse to be away from *Sunday Style* for long enough to meet him.

Claire was starting to give me more things to do for her. She reckoned I had good judgement for what readers would be interested in, and what was complete rubbish. Since last week I'd been opening her post each day. You'd never believe the amount of ridiculous stuff and waste of paper a Beauty editor gets sent. Press releases announcing new products, new shop-openings, new ranges, new brands, new books, new research . . . Samples of every kind of cosmetic you can think of . . . Baskets of fruit and bunches of flowers, keyrings and perfume bottles, silk scarves and boxes of shells and sand (why? Don't ask me). For some reason PRs seem to think these gifts and gimmicks will make editors more inclined to write about their products in the magazine.

That morning, I'd collected together all the stuff that had accumulated over the past few weeks and Claire didn't want, and now we were having a Beauty Sale. I'd emailed everyone in the Sunday and Saturday magazine offices: '2.30 p.m. – Beauty Sale, *Sunday Style*. Bring an empty make-up bag and a full purse. All takings to Breast Cancer Care.'

The goods were in two big cardboard boxes, with the choicest pickings laid out across a table next to the subs that's usually scattered with magazines and proofs.

Come 2.15, our office was filling up with faces (mainly

female) that I didn't recognise. Word must have travelled down to the paper.

'It's one of the highlights of office life,' explained Claire. 'Top cosmetic brands for a few pence. And there's nothing like a good sale scrum, is there? Digging in and elbowing your way through to the best buys.' She laughed.

Jan was there too, rummaging around and stacking up her spoils. I wouldn't have thought she needed to scrimp on cosmetics. Surely editors earned decent money.

I'd decided to hold back and let others fight it out for the Dior and the Bobbi Brown. If I'm really, truthfully honest, I find make-up a little intimidating. Like I've said, I'm never sure I'm putting it on right. But Claire had cast an expert's eye over my skin and colouring and picked out a small selection for me before the sale. Now Nita added a beautiful teal blue eyeshadow ('You'll look stunning in that.' 'Yeah, but how do I put it on so I don't look like Car Crash Barbie?').

The sale was winding down, only the unappetising crumbs left after the locusts had feasted. People drifted off back to their desks or out to the lift.

'Time to count up,' said Claire, emptying a heap of coins from paper coffee cups on to her desk.

'Five pounds, six pounds, eight pounds . . .' I was checking the takings when Ben called. Or, in fact, texted. He wanted to meet right away.

'Is it all right if I finish this later, Claire? I need to take something to the Post Office today, before it closes.'

She smiled. 'You could put it in our "out tray", if you like.'
I glanced over at the wire racks where the post was collected.

'No. Thanks. I'd prefer to take it myself. It's important.
Something my dad left behind at the flat.' I couldn't believe
how easily the lie was coming out of my mouth. I try not to
tell porkies if I can help it. I know politicians lie all the time,
but I wanted to be someone who exposed the truth, not
covered it up.

I rushed towards the doors before Claire could say
anything else and I could dig myself even deeper. I
wondered what she must be thinking of me.

Just as I was leaving, Jan called from her office door:
'Claire, can I have a word? I've an idea about something.'

I glanced back over my shoulder and caught Jan's eye.
She was looking straight at me. I smiled at her – well, you do
when it's your boss, don't you? (Or certainly if you want to
get on.) She looked puzzled. Oh no – she was probably
wondering where I was going too.

My heart was pounding in the lift down. I could hear this
sloosh, sloosh noise in my ears. I put my hand in my bag for
about the fiftieth time to check that my dictaphone was
there. And my headphones.

Marble steps with a steel handrail led down from the
atrium with the lifts to the ground-floor level below. Looking
over the edge I could see from above that Ben was at a table
by the Costa coffee bar, near the exit to the square. I trotted
halfway down the stairs and then stopped. Perhaps I
shouldn't have bothered showing the transcript to Ben after

all. I mean, it wasn't like he was going to suddenly know exactly what The Conversation was all about. He might catch a few things that I'd missed – I supposed he might recognise a word or phrase that in my typing was written as: 'xxxxxxxxxxx what does this mean????? can't hear?????.'

Maybe I should dash (quietly) back up the stairs before he saw me, text to apologise for not meeting and tell him to forget all about it. I'd go back to concentrating on *Sunday Style* – which I was enjoying more now – and try harder to come up with ideas that would make my name in the magazine.

But I carried on walking down. Sally would say it was because I was in denial about fancying Ben and wanted desperately to impress him. I would say it was because I needed to see if my story 'had legs' (as they say for some reason in journalism) and wanted desperately to impress him.

'Hi,' I said, brightly and breathily. Ben had his head down, reading the transcript on top of a newspaper.

'Hi there, Becky.' He looked up with a smile. His eyes were grey. Definitely a deep grey. 'D'you want a coffee or anything? Juice? Water?'

'No thanks. I'm fine.' I fiddled with my belt buckle, like I do when I'm nervous.

'Shall we go and see if this recording's going to bring down the government?'

I grinned. 'I don't think it'll quite do that . . .'

'Well, you never know . . . You've heard of Watergate, haven't you? Woodward and Bernstein?'

'Kind of.' I knew that two journalists in the US in the 1970s had helped uncover a scandal that led to the president of the time, Richard Nixon, resigning. 'It was those two journalists, wasn't it? I think my parents went to see the film . . .'

I wasn't sure what else to say, so I stared down at my feet. My hair was over my eyes.

'That's right. They dared to publish and forced a corrupt president to resign,' Ben intoned with mock drama. I wasn't sure if he was teasing me or if he really thought this story could be big. He closed the flap of his bag and put it over his shoulder. 'Let's go outside, get some rays while I take a listen.'

We pushed open the glazed double doors, one handle each. The glass was tinted and outside it was blindingly bright in contrast. My eyes watered and I reached for my sunglasses. But I couldn't feel them in my bag. Ben screwed up his face against the light.

I rummaged in my bag some more and closed my fingers around my shades. It was better with them on. I could relax my eyes and hide behind the darkened lenses. I tossed my hair, aware that people would be seeing Ben Hutchison and a 'mystery honey-blonde' (they wouldn't be mean and say 'mousey' would they?) walking across the grass. I wished I felt better in the clothes I was wearing.

'You know, Becky, seriously, we may not find anything on this recording that we can use. You do realise that, don't you?'

'Yeah. Of course,' I said. 'I know it's probably nothing. But, you know, I had this feeling when the bloke was talking—'

'No, I'm sure your instincts are good. It's just that if we can't identify the man it could all lead to a dead end.' Ben glanced over to make sure I was taking this in. 'I've been thinking, though . . .'

What had he been thinking? My chest did one of those little leaps, and I tried to look even cooler behind my sunglasses.

'. . . there are other stories you could help me with writing. If you fancy that. You know, like with background research on Westminster – you must hear a lot about how things work there.'

He wanted me to carry on helping him – even if my story came to nothing. That was what I'd wanted to hear. 'Definitely. I'd really like to work with you some more. Though it's my dad you should ask about Westminster. He'd have lots of stories.'

'I bet he would!' laughed Ben.

'Here?' I asked. We'd been strolling across the lawn but now seemed a good time to sit down. I was desperate to find out if Ben knew who the man in the suit was.

He plugged my earphones into his ears and fumbled with the dictaphone controls. I had to reach over and press the right buttons to start it playing – my pale, short-nailed fingers next to his tanned, nail-bitten ones.

11

I was ecstatic all the way up in the lift, all the way through the magazine floor reception, all the way through the glass doors. Right until I saw Alison's face.

She beckoned urgently. 'Where have you been?' she asked in a raised whisper as I reached her desk. 'You've been away ages and Claire was about to send out a search party. Nita said you were with Ben. Is that right? She gave me your number and Claire and I both tried calling you.'

'Yes . . .' I hadn't realised my absence would cause such a fuss. I hadn't been gone that long, had I? 'I was talking to him about a story – I was fine. Sorry. I didn't mean to make anyone worry. I just didn't want Claire to think I'm not interested in the magazine and that I was, like, bunking off my placement here.'

'I understand,' said Alison. 'I'm glad you're OK, but you'd better go and sort things out with Claire. Go on, now – get it over with.' Alison almost pushed me over in Claire's direction.

Sheepishly, I made my way to Claire's desk. It faces away from the door, and she hadn't seen me come in. But I felt as though everyone else in the room had their eyes glued to me.

'Claire?'

She turned around. 'Becky? So you're all right. What were you thinking? Why didn't you answer your phone?'

'I'm really sorry, Claire. I didn't hear it. I was with—'

'I know where you were, Becky. Thanks to Nita. Please, just don't do that again. London is . . . Well, it's not always safe to be out on your own. Things happen that you read about in the papers, or hear from people. We were worried. You were away for an hour and a half.'

I coloured up. So it had been that long. Claire seemed more stressed than angry. Still, I couldn't have felt much worse or more humiliated if she'd shouted at me.

'I'm sorry, Claire. I promise I won't do that again. I'll let you know where I am in future, or how long I'm going to be.'

'Thanks – we don't want to have to worry about you.' Claire took a deep breath and looked me straight in the face. 'Look, Becky, you're seventeen and it's not down to me to tell you where you should be or how to behave – I'm not your parents or anything. But Jan talked to me just as you were going out about giving you some more writing and editorial experience in your time here. This could be a fantastic chance, if you're as serious as you seem to be about a career in journalism. It's up to you if you want to do some extra things for the paper in your own time – but if you don't take up the opportunities here on the magazine, then you'll find they probably won't be offered again. OK?'

I nodded. I felt small and suddenly stupid. Was I messing

up my chances on the magazine by sneaking off to Ben and the paper? But I wanted the magazine *and* my story with Ben. Couldn't I do both? My nose started to sting.

'Can I go to the toilet?'

Claire laughed. 'We're not at school, are we? Go on. It'll all be fine, don't worry. Come back after the loo and we can talk about what exciting projects I'm lining up for you.'

In the toilets I had stern words with myself: 'I am not going to cry. I am not going to cry. There's nothing to cry about.' Mum says I'm oversensitive, but she can talk . . . I dabbed at the corners of my eyes with a piece of loo paper. I was OK. Things were fine. Things were more than fine – they were incredible.

When Ben had started listening to the tape he'd made a strange kind of face. His mouth opened and then closed and his eyebrows went up and then furrowed down. He sat up, cross-legged on the grass, placed both hands over his ears and bent his head. He had a few days of stubble, pale brown and glinting golden in places. On the back of his hand my number was smudged, but still there.

He pulled the headphones out of his ears. 'I know who it is,' he said. 'Becky, do you realise what this means? I've – we've – got a story! I know who it is!'

'Really? You're sure?'

I'd so been preparing myself for disappointment that it took a while to sink in.

'I can prove it to you. Come on. I've got an idea.' He

pulled me up by the hand and we ran across the lawn. Ben was almost shouting, excitedly: 'This is what it's supposed to feel like – getting the lead that's going to put my name on the front page.'

My breath came fast from our sprint to the glass doors. Inside it was cool and dark. 'Where are we going?'

'Up to my desk. Or any computer will do.'

He punched the floor number in the lift.

At his desk he did an image search: *"james hepworth" auricle.* The screen filled with a gallery of photos and captions. He scanned through them and then clicked on one. 'Tell me if that's the man you saw on the train.'

I leaned across.

It was him. The man in The Conversation. The one I'd heard saying all those things.

'That's him,' I said to Ben. I could hardly believe it. 'I'm pretty sure. No, definitely. It is. Are there other pictures?' I wanted to be totally certain, as sure as if I were picking him out in an identity parade.

Ben clicked up a few more. There was no mistake.

'So who is he?'

'James Hepworth. He works for a company called Auricle – he's their PR. He used to be a political lobbyist, which is where I've come across him, and then he was poached by one of his clients. Gold. That's what he does.'

'You mean bullion, like Fort Knox?'

'Kind of. Auricle's a precious metals refiner. They supply some of the biggest names on the high street.'

'So why would they need a political lobbyist to do their PR?'

'Because gold's a hot subject these days. You've heard of Dirty Gold, right?'

I remembered something about it in the 'ethical consumer' section of one of the Sunday papers. It had taken oven from Conflict Diamonds as the big mining scandal. 'I've read a bit about it,' I said.

'Becky, if this is a cover-up about dirty gold, this story could be . . .' Ben grinned and winked at me, '. . . pure gold dust.'

'So what do we do now?'

'Well, I don't want to confront James or anyone else at Auricle until we've got more facts, and worked out what it is he's trying to hide. I'm going to make a few calls this afternoon. How about you do some research on the net to give me some background? That sound OK to you, Becks?'

He'd called me the nickname my friends use. It must mean he felt comfortable with me.

We agreed I'd come in early the next day, and work late too, after my hours on *Sunday Style*. Then Ben kissed me goodbye on the cheek: 'See you tomorrow. I'll keep you up to date if I find anything.' Like I said, I was ecstatic when I got upstairs.

Blog for Monday 28 July:

one of the most exciting days of my life
so far! I am working on this extremely
secret story with ben which i'd love to
tell you about but it's just too secret,
maybe i'll be able to say more another
time. ben n i are becoming friends i
think. tho i'm still not sure - maybe i
want it to be more. he has lovely eyes -
did i say that before? n i am so fed up
with boys my own age. anyway he's already
kissed me. sure it was just one of those
friendly-on-the-cheek kisses but it was
still a kiss.

jake called me like a good chaperone but
it was only to tempt me out! i'd been
having a really s*!*t afternoon on sunday
style because of skipping off to see ben
but then jake cheered me up by saying he
was meeting some mates in camden n wud i
like to come? so at last my london social
life is getting more interesting.

nita n i also had invites to a shop launch
in primrose hill (which is very near
camden) so we thought we cud go n meet jake

afterwards. at the shop they were serving glasses of champagne as soon as we got in through the door. we grabbed two each to make sure we didn't miss out but it's hard trying to look through clothes rails when both your hands are full so we ended up glugging them down really quickly.

the launch was packed n tallulah the fashion editor kept trying to introduce us to people. she was being v sweet but v hyper. we kept having to hide over the other side of the shop to avoid having to talk to people we didn't know. nita n i decided to escape into the changing rooms. nita chose loads of stuff for me n said we shd do a makeover. she wudn't even let me see what she'd picked. i pulled out a few things for her too for a laugh - the most expensive and outrageous.

we made so much noise in the changing rooms i'm surprised we weren't thrown out. the woman in charge looked a bit tense at first but we promised to be really careful with the clothes. nita looked like a film star in this amazing pink dress. i loved everything she chose for me except a blue shift that made my knees look knobbly. there were two tops i really really wanted but even with the launch discount the shop was still way more expensive than i'd usually pay so i wasn't sure.

but i told nita about my taxi money stash n she said i'd be mad not to spend it on something that made me look fabulous. n then tallulah got me an even bigger discount. i was so pleased i went n gave her a big hug (i was a bit drunk by now too).

then we went to meet jake. he was at a bar called the railway tavern. we sat up on the roof terrace and looked down on everyone walking by below. all the goths n emos. jake introduced us to his mates who are in a band that he says are going to be the 'next big thing'.

rich n manny's band is called sharpedge. rich was nice i suppose. he has dark curly hair n dark brown eyes and was very intense. they invited us to a gig at the end of the week. rich said their music is inspired by 80s bands like the jam and the 60s mod sound. they're playing at the V festival at the end of august - sally n i wanted to go to that anyway (parents permitting)! it'd be fantastic if nita cud come too. partway through the evening i had a call from mum and had to pretend i wasn't in a pub. jake spoke to her n swore that he'd taken me out to a pizza place - which was cool! when it was closing time jake n his friends walked me n nita to the tube station. it took ages to get down on the northern line. i kept falling asleep n being scared i wud miss my stop. when i got out at oval i had a txt from ben saying c u tomorrow 8.30. b. no kisses but i went to bed a very happy grrrl.

12

The alarm clock drilled itself through my head. Why had I set it so early? Oh yeah, I remembered . . . I had an appointment at 8.30 a.m. An appointment with a certain Mr Ben Gorgeous Hutchison. Except that right at this moment I felt far from gorgeous myself. My eyes were fat and sore and my head was fuzzy. I pulled myself upright. Oh no, not a good idea. Defeated by the vertical, I flopped back down.

I'd managed not to get drunk up till now during my London stay. But then, of course, Dad had been in the flat and looking over me. My first night of freedom and I'd got slaughtered. Mind you, I had two fantastic tops to show for it.

The snooze on the alarm rammed another hole through my head. 'Bugger off!' I swept it off the table and slunk back under the covers. I tell you, if this had been for anyone else than Ben and anything less than the Biggest Story of My Life then I wouldn't have made it beyond the end of my bed all day.

I was running late. No time for a shower. Breakfast didn't happen – I wasn't even hungry. I slung on the nearest clothes

I could find (I'd left the bag with all my clean ones at the office when I went out partying), then hesitated over the fancy carrier bag from Zina Q. Should I bring out one of my new tops? I had a look at both, rolled one up as carefully as I could manage in its tissue paper, and bunged it in my shoulder bag.

At Canary Wharf the bankers were strutting through the already bright day. Journalists, I'd found, tended to make a later start. Late nights in the office and the effects of alcohol, I figured.

Ben ushered me into the newspaper office. There was a hush about the place. A few other people were here early, bent in concentration over their computer screens, steaming paper cups of coffee on their desks. A croissant here and there, or yogurt and muesli in a plastic tub. I could have done with a coffee, but food was still off my personal agenda.

'You can sit in the usual place.'

'Richard still away then?'

'For another week. I think.'

I was moving very slowly and deliberately, not wanting to induce any more of the feelings of nausea that had made the Tube ride a torture this morning. Ben must have noticed.

'You OK there? You look a bit . . . delicate?'

'Mm.'

'I've got some paracetamol. Want one?'

'Thank you. Yes. I am suffering, just a bit. If you see me any time wanting more than two glasses of champagne, please stop me by any means you have to.'

Ben grinned and I grinned back.

'Champagne. That's a bad one. I can drink anything else, but not champagne. Three glasses and I'm rolling on the floor,' he said.

'I'd like to see that,' I said, brightening a little.

'Well, you never know – if this story has the wings I think it has, we may both be rolling on the floor.' Ben stopped and looked hurriedly down. He must have realised what he'd said. 'So . . .' he continued after a pause. 'Shall we get started, then? I phoned a contact – someone I trust – at Cafod yesterday and they had some interesting ideas about what your conversation could have been about.'

Ben filled me in on what he'd discovered and I typed notes to remind myself. Cafod was a charity that, among other things, was running a campaign to raise awareness about dirty gold, and persuade all UK retailers to sign up to a pledge that they would work with their suppliers to ensure the gold they used was mined ethically, and without huge environmental damage.

In the US, Ben continued, it was Oxfam who ran the No Dirty Gold campaign. 'NDG,' I typed. NDG. NDG. Endejiahs! I'd thought Mr Pinstripe – James Hepworth – was talking about something in Arabic, like the mujahideen, but really it was NDGers – No Dirty Gold campaigners. 'That's it! The thing he's hiding is something the No Dirty Gold campaign mustn't find out about.'

'Something that would be a PR disaster,' finished Ben. 'So have there been any stories recently that mention Auricle or any of its clients? I made a client list yesterday – here it is. OK, Becks, as well as background on dirty gold, can you check online for stories with anything about Auricle. Let's say in the past six months. And I'll check out their clients.'

In the next half-hour I bookmarked all the recent articles, press releases and blog and forum mentions I could find. I emailed the list of links to Ben, and also to myself, so I could carry on in spare moments upstairs.

'It's my time to go to the other place,' I said at 9.30.

'Up to the fabulous world of fashion, eh?' said Ben. I'd confided my ambivalence about working for a style magazine to him. But he also knew I didn't want to mess things up if I was getting chances there.

'That's right. Better not be late. See you after school – work, I mean.' We'd decided my lunchtime flits downstairs weren't such a great idea: we'd get more done and more uninterrupted time if we worked in the evenings.

'Thanks, Becky,' Ben added as I was picking up my things.

'What for?'

'For trusting me with this. Bringing me the story.'

I felt a glow. But also a sneaking feeling of unease. Wasn't this supposed to be *my* story?

Sarah breezed up to her desk as I was leaving and gave me a funny look. 'Hi, Becky. Can't seem to keep you away, can we?'

She put her head close to Ben's and whispered something. They both laughed and looked at each other.

* * *

I grumped about all morning. I was suffering, despite the painkillers, and I couldn't help running that image of Ben and Sarah over and over in my head.

Looking at some of the links about dirty gold made me feel small and petty. It kind of put things in perspective. The issue was big news in the United States because of the gold mining there. Environmental damage from mine construction. Most gold was extracted by trickling cyanide down through a mountain of gold ore – leaving massively poisonous chemicals as a result. Contaminated drinking water. Displaced communities. Toxic waste left from the mining process, even after the mines closed – up to thirty tonnes of it for just one ounce of gold (enough for a chunky ring). Gold extraction was possibly the world's most polluting industry. It made me want to give up buying gold jewellery straight away.

And then I started reading the pages about the Democratic Republic of Congo. There was a report saying that gold had fuelled fighting and war crimes there – armed groups battled for control of the mines, and got weapons in exchange for gold smuggled out of the country. People work in the mines to feed their families, but the wages are low and it's incredibly dangerous. Congo's gold could make the country comfortable for all its inhabitants, but corruption – including by international mining companies – and conflict have meant it's brought misery instead. Or that seemed to be the conclusion of the articles I was reading. There was some hope, but reforms by the government and mining companies were happening only slowly.

I nearly jumped when Claire placed the coffee tray down in front of me; I'd been in another, much darker, world. Her gesture meant it was my turn to do the coffee round for the Fashion and Beauty desks. Alison was heading out with a tray to look after the subs and Design, so I caught up with her.

'You're looking a bit the worse for wear,' she said. 'Late night, was it?'

'Something like that,' I replied, not completely returned from Congo yet. 'Nita and I went to that opening – Tallulah's friend's shop – and then we met up with my cousin Jake in Camden.'

'Camden? I haven't been there in ages. Not really my scene these days. Too many unwashed students with too many piercings.'

'I liked it,' I said, feeling a little defensive. I didn't have any piercings, apart from my ears, but I was certainly unwashed this morning.

'What's this story you're working on with Ben? You were spotted with your heads together this morning.'

I wasn't sure how much I wanted to tell Alison. It wasn't that I didn't trust her – after all, she'd helped me write up Dan's story and hadn't stolen that, so she'd hardly try to nick this one. But it was mine and Ben's story, you know? I was happy with it being the two of us and I didn't want to include anyone else. I liked it being a secret – for now.

'It's just something I found. It could be quite big but we don't know yet. I can't really say much at the moment. It's at a sensitive stage.'

'A sensitive stage? OK, it's all right, you don't have to tell me if you don't want to,' said Alison. 'Three cappuccinos, an espresso and two normal teas, please,' she added to the server at the canteen coffee bar. 'I was interested, that's all,' she said to me again. Was she a bit jealous, perhaps?

Alison waited while I got my order too, and we walked back together along the corridor to the office. I was trying another espresso today – perhaps it would give me a jolt and zap the hangover. I was also drinking gallons of water; I was so thirsty.

'There's a shower on this floor, you know,' said Alison. 'I sometimes find that helps if I'm the worse for wear. I can lend you a towel.'

So that lunchtime I bought a razor along with my cheese sarnie and went to have a shower. It felt so good. Hot water spiking down on me. Alison's towel was fluffy and freshly washed. I put on the new top I'd brought. It was green and white, with this great abstract pattern. Very 60s. I was glad I'd bundled it into my bag – well, I was going to be spending several hours with Ben Hutchison later on.

I did as 'Edie' a pose as I could manage, held my phone at arm's length and messaged a photo to Sally – we always compare new outfits. She was 'bored as f*!*', she texted back, and couldn't wait to see Steve.

Back in the office there were plenty of comments

about my lunchtime transformation. I was sooo glad Nita had talked me into my purchases. She was looking brilliant as usual, and she didn't seem to be suffering like me. Lucky cow!

Tuesday was a busy day on the magazine – a press day. That's when the computer files with the pages are sent to the printer. There was a hush of concentration as subs and editors read proofs and made corrections. Alison had explained to me all about how the magazine works in my first few days at *Sunday Style*.

Each week, at the editorial meeting, the editors of the different parts of the magazine (Features, Beauty, etc.) all talk about the mix of articles and fashion stories that will go in that issue. They're sent millions of ideas by PRs and freelance writers (most of them rubbish, says Alison), and they look at what's in other magazines, or what they've thought up themselves. Then they either write the articles themselves or get someone on the paper to do them, or a freelancer who works for lots of different publications.

'And then when the articles have come in, and the section editors have had their go at them . . .' Alison had explained, stopping to take a swig of her orange juice, which left a tiny orange moustache, '. . . then, we take over and get down to the detail work.' She meant making sure it all made sense and was spelled properly. Then she and the other subs would suggest a selection of headlines to Jan and Felicity to choose between.

When the picture editor and researchers have got the

photos together, and the designers have designed the pages, the article goes back around to the subs again for 'cutting and polishing', as Alison puts it. Which means cutting out words and paragraphs so the article is the right length, and proofreading it.

None of this had meant a lot to me at the time. It swooshed over my head as I tried to remember people's names, the layout of the office, and how to log on to the computer. But now I was getting the hang of the weekly rhythm. Monday, with the editorial meeting for the next week's magazine cutting into the proofreading and making the subs jumpy. The last pages for the coming Sunday's mag going to the printers on a Tuesday. Wednesday slower and sleepier – people recovering from what was often a late night the day before, as everyone struggled to keep to the deadline set by the printers. Thursday and Friday gearing up again for the big push of producing the magazine.

Next week would be my last on *Sunday Style* – and the paper. And there was so much I still wanted to do in that time. (Including working on Mum and Dad some more to persuade them that staying on in London on my own was a great idea, and not something they needed to hold an international summit about.)

Jan had said she'd like Nita and me to write at least one article that could be published in the magazine before we left. Alison told me that this is, like, really unusual, and that we shouldn't get depressed if Jan didn't use them in the end, or if she rewrote them so much that we couldn't spot any words that were actually ours. I like to think Jan had been impressed by me getting Dan's story into the main paper, and that it had made her look twice at us work experiencers.

Claire sat down with me yesterday, as she had promised, and we figured out what I was going to write about. We decided to turn my idea about taking parabens out of cosmetics into a 'good news' story rather than something that might scare off the advertisers (and without the advertisers the magazine wouldn't exist). I could write about brands that were deciding to 'go natural' and organic. Why didn't I take a long weekend – interview the founders of the Midford Vale Eco Spa on Friday and take a photographer along? I chewed on my pen when Claire mentioned this idea and didn't reply at first. I felt awkward about going into what I regarded as my mum's territory – asking her to sort something out for me.

'But if you've got the contact, why not use it?' Claire replied.

She had a point. I was being stupid. And my mum knew other eco-brand people too. It was just the thought of her being so smug at my actually coming to her to ask for help that held me back.

When I was fifteen Matt told me a secret. I still don't absolutely know if it's true. It was a secret about me, and I suppose I could ask Mum or Dad straight out about it. But I never have.

I'd been giving Matt a hard time about how disappointed

Dad and Mum were that he was looking as though he was going to flunk his A-levels and get into, like, none of his uni choices. I realised at the time I was going on and on, being a bitch. But I couldn't help myself. He can be so arrogant, it really pisses me off.

So then suddenly he says he knows something that he hasn't told me before because he didn't want to hurt me. (Meaning he did want to hurt me now?) He said he'd overheard Mum and Dad arguing a month or two before. Mum was screaming and Dad was doing what he does, which is to not get angry but sulk instead. In the part of the argument that Matt heard they were rowing about money, and about Mum having given up her career to look after us, and something about supporting Dad and didn't he realise how tough it had been on her, and how with 'all this new trouble to cope with' she was nearly at breaking point.

And then Mum said something about me. She shouted that Dad knew I'd been a mistake. That she'd never wanted another child.

I didn't speak to Matt for the rest of the day. Maybe Mum hadn't said that at all, and he'd misheard. Or perhaps she didn't mean it like it came out. After all, as Sally pointed out, plenty of children are 'mistakes' that their parents haven't planned, but that doesn't mean they don't love them.

13

Ben was standing talking to someone, facing the office doors. I was walking along the aisle between the desks and the wall. There were still lots of journalists here, as there were every night. Upstairs I'd left everyone frantically trying to finish this week's magazine, but there wasn't much I could do to help. Nita had offered to stay behind and do some proofreading. Spelling's not one of the things I'm good at.

So I was walking towards Ben, and his colleague, and they turned to look in my direction. The other guy was still trying to hold a conversation, but he wasn't getting any reply. It was as though Ben couldn't take his eyes off me. As though he was mesmerised. I couldn't be sure, but that was how it looked.

'Hi, Becky,' he said, and his dark grey eyes looked different; warmer, more flirty. 'I like that top – it really suits you.'

'Thanks,' I said.

Ben turned to his workmate. 'I'll fill you in on more later – or tomorrow, OK?'

'Fine, mate,' came the response. And Ben's colleague

smiled at me in a not entirely innocent way. 'Bye, Becky, see you 'round,' he said.

Ben had been emailing me updates through the afternoon. He'd checked up on Auricle's clients, looked up the company's latest accounts and report and asked the Economics correspondent to interpret them. He'd followed up with his Cafod contact and looked at the recent article links I'd sent about Auricle. And now he thought that perhaps, maybe, he had discovered what it was that James Hepworth was trying so hard to cover up.

'A number of jewellery brands and retailers – the outlets on the high street, right – have signed up to this pledge to make sure they trade ethically, and their gold isn't from mines with bad safety or environmental records, or that sort of thing. If I'm being cynical, it's because they don't want that to impact on their sales and their brand image. If I'm being kinder, it's because they do actually care about where their gold comes from and simply hadn't thought about it too deeply before. So, given that, why would Auricle be really, really keen to keep something hidden from the No Dirty Gold campaign – and everybody else, for that matter?'

I opened my mouth to try and make a stab at the answer, but then Ben piled in: 'Because,' he said, 'some of their gold is dodgy, and one of their clients has sworn blind it's not, and they don't want to lose that client and they don't want to lose face. So the only answer is to make absolutely sure nobody finds out about it.'

I thought I followed his argument. 'So which client

is it, then?' I couldn't believe we were about to crack The Conversation.

'This one,' said Ben, bringing up a web page on his computer. 'I'm dead certain – well, nearly dead certain.'

The site for Lina flashed up on the screen.

'Lina! Their jewellery's, like, in all the fashion magazines. There's some in next week's *Sunday Style*. Everyone wears it – I mean, loads of film and music stars.'

'Right. And would someone like Madonna want to know that her favourite jewellery has been funding civil war in the Democratic Republic of Congo? I don't think so.'

It was a strange feeling: so this was it, then? This was what The Conversation had been about – what James Hepworth had discussed so indiscreetly on the train. Lina was using dirty gold, but didn't know it. And Auricle needed to cover it up. Most people in the street might not really know about dirty gold, but stars like Bob Geldof, or Bono, or George Clooney were known for making a fuss about such things.

'So what do we do now?' I asked.

'We make the story stick. We tie everything up as far as we can, throw in lots of names of celebrities and quotes if we can – you can look after that side – expose Auricle for what they're doing, and make dirty gold front-page news. So long as nothing else comes along to knock it off, of course. Like a general election or a terrorist plot or a missing child.'

It all sounded fantastic. Except that suddenly it didn't feel so much like my story any more. I'd brought it to Ben because I couldn't get any further, but it was still disappointing that I hadn't been the one to find the jigsaw piece that fitted it all together. Maybe – I couldn't help thinking – if I hadn't had to spend hours on the phone to my mum setting up interviews and stuff for *Sunday Style* (and reassuring her that, yes, I was fine, and no, I wasn't staying out too late) and instead studied those article links more closely, I might have spotted that piece about Lina myself. The one where they boasted how they'd persuaded their supplier to source only responsibly mined gold from now on.

'That's great,' I said. 'So what do we do now?'

It wasn't that I didn't want my *Sunday Style* article to work out – it would be brilliant to have that too – but this story meant so much more. It was more, like, serious, you know? It could make a difference. It could change the way people thought, and maybe even help to make things better in a country that I'd only ever seen on the news.

'We try to speak to James Hepworth – though I doubt we'll get anything more than "No comment" or something bland and corporate – and then we write the article.' Ben lifted his coffee cup. 'Cheers, Becks – you done good. We should go out and celebrate later. And I s'pose I'd better talk to Stephen . . .' Ben swivelled his head, trying to spy the small, dark-haired figure of the paper's editor. He was with the designers, pointing to a headline and picture on the computer screen and disagreeing loudly with what the designer was saying ' Maybe I'll wait till tomorrow morning's meeting,' Ben concluded.

He told me what I needed to do to write up the information I'd found about dirty gold, then he put in his phone call to Mr Pinstripe.

I got to work, like a real pro. I was excited, heart racing, that a story I'd found could be so important – even if I hadn't found the crucial missing link. It was something I couldn't have dreamed of a few weeks ago (although, in fact, I *had* dreamed about it in recent days – including the celebration afterwards with Ben). But did this mean that my adventure with Ben was nearly over? What if there were no more stories to work on together before the end of my placement?

When he got off the phone Ben stared at the handset, as though he didn't know what it was. 'Amazing. James Hepworth's agreed to an interview,' he said.

The pub faced on to the water. People crowded outside in huddles of work colleagues; inside the hard surfaces magnified the buzz of many conversations. It had floor-to-ceiling windows and rectangular wooden tables that were past the new and shiny phase of their life: the surfaces were marked with grooves and cigarette marks, and pale rings from the thousands of drinks that had stood on them.

'Over here,' said Ben, pointing towards a corner where a group of people from the paper were already sitting. I could see Sarah's blonde head among them. She noticed us and smiled and waved at Ben. We went and pulled up chairs next to her.

'What can I get you, Becky?' Ben asked. 'You legal yet?'

'I'm still seventeen,' I replied.

'I suppose I should be responsible and stick to getting you something non-alcoholic, then. But if I got a spare glass of wine, and you happened to have a sip of it now and again . . . That wouldn't do any harm, would it?'

'I'll have an orange juice, but I'm not sure I . . .'

'Anyone else need a top-up?'

Ben can't have heard my uncertainty. It didn't matter. I could just leave the wine. I'd got over feeling ill but I didn't think I wanted to repeat it all tonight. Ben threw a cluster of crisp packets on to the table.

'That's supper sorted then,' said one of the other journalists.

For a while I sipped my juice and looked around and listened. I recognised a couple of other faces, but that was it. Everyone was talking loudly and drinking quickly. Some people were moaning about their jobs and the paper; others were discussing stories they were working on, or house prices in London, or where they were going or had been on holiday. There wasn't anything I could really join in. I sat some more and sipped some more orange juice. Someone else got a round, and another orange juice and another glass of wine appeared in front of me. Perhaps a few mouthfuls would be OK?

The man behind the bar looked over in my direction and said something to the journalist buying the drinks as he handed over his change. 'No mate, it's fine, she's eighteen.

'Course you have to ask, but it's fine, honest.'

The journalist leaned over my shoulder when he came back. His breath was beery. 'If the barman comes and asks your age, say you're eighteen but you've forgotten your ID, right? I just told him you're OK to drink.' He squeezed back into his seat and winked at me.

I decided not to have any wine after all. I didn't want to get Ben or anyone in trouble.

Ben smiled over. 'You OK?' He'd been taking centre stage, keeping people amused by telling funny stories about weird things that had happened to him: 'There was this time when . . .'

'Yeah, I'm good,' I replied. But then he turned away again.

Sarah was talking to him about something, but it was impossible to hear what they were saying over the noise. I couldn't work out if I liked Sarah or not. She kept putting her hand on Ben's arm.

Then Alison came in and stood at the door a moment, turning her head around and looking to see who was here.

I jumped up and waved at her. No one else seemed to have noticed her come in. She beamed over.

'Hi, Becky. Can I make space next to you?'

I manoeuvred my chair so there was room for her to pull up another. Ben and Sarah were sitting on a bench seat on the other side of the table now.

I was pleased to see Alison. At last someone I could have a conversation with. 'How's it been on the magazine?'

It was after nine o'clock, but I knew that was pretty early for a press day.

'Oh, I've been given the evening off. Andy and Nicky are staying this time around. Everything's coming through so slowly there's no point having all of us there. They reckon it's going to be a late one.'

'Jan?'

'You guessed. She wanted to change around all the features, got the designers reworking at least one of them, said she wasn't happy with the layout. And there's another one she's rewriting herself almost from scratch. I feel sorry for Emma sometimes. It's not exactly going to build your self-esteem, being Features editor on *Sunday Style*.'

As she spoke to me, Alison's eyes kept flicking over towards Ben and Sarah. When Sarah got up to go to the toilet, Alison moved herself round to sit next to Ben. And I was all on my own again.

People kept disappearing off to the loos, sometimes in pairs. Not everyone in the group, but a few. They'd exchange glances, and then reach under the table, or pass a wallet between them, and head off. They weren't so obvious as to come back sniffing, or wiping their noses, like you see on TV. They probably thought I didn't know what they were doing, but I'm not that naïve.

No school wants to admit its pupils have anything to do with drugs. But it happens. Sally and I had a drag of skunk once, but it made me feel sick. I really thought I was going to throw up. The boy who offered it to us laughed, and said we'd get used to it if we carried on. But I didn't want to find out.

Sometimes you see people hanging around together, standing close in a quiet part of town, or walking along a street and passing something in their palms. Sometimes it's even people who hate each other normally. And then you really know it's got to be something to do with drugs.

When Sarah came back she sat in Alison's seat, next to me, and I could even see her hand under the table, fumbling as she tried to pass the little paper packet to Ben. But he shook his head and kept both hands on the table, round his pint. Alison mouthed 'No thanks' too. She was facing towards Ben, with her head close to his. Her eyes were glittering and they were sharing some kind of joke, or story. He kept looking at her and at one point he took her hand and looked at the palm and they both laughed.

I talked to Sarah for a while (she was very talkative) and to some of the other people round the table. When Alison got up for her round I said I just wanted a glass of water. Sarah took over my spare glasses of wine – after two extras people must have noticed I wasn't drinking, so they stopped buying them. The table reached its peak volume, with people almost shouting, and waving their arms as they spoke. And then there were consultations about time and the chairs started to empty. There were lots of 'See you tomorrows'.

Maybe I'd better go myself, I thought. I picked up my bag.

I don't know if Ben saw that I was getting ready to leave, but he came round to sit by me. He'd hardly spoken to me all evening. 'Sorry, Becks, I've been caught up with other people. I know it was supposed to be our celebration. D'you fancy getting something to eat? I really should eat something, and I can't let you go home hungry. There's a tapas place round the corner. My treat.'

'I should probably get back to the flat,' I said. I was feeling pouty. Sarah and Alison obviously both had the hots for Ben, and even if I was interested (Sally would snort at this point and say that obviously I was), why would he look at me rather than one of them?

'I'll make sure you get home safely. What do you say?'

I thought about it for a millisecond. 'OK.'

Alison and Sarah were standing by the pub door with their coats on. Ben explained he was taking me out for supper. They smiled and nodded as though it was all fine and they weren't bothered. Sarah waved and Alison came up and gave me a hug and a kiss on the cheek. 'Night, Becky – don't stay out too late will you! And you' – she prodded Ben in the chest – 'make sure you look after Becky. Remember she's only seventeen.'

I'd told Mum and Jake that I was working late on a story then going home straight afterwards. Which was true at the time I told them. It was just that plans had changed.

Outside it was getting dark, but the air was still warmish. There was a light breeze and the sound of voices and music on the air. People were out on the streets, coming out of pubs and bars, like us, wandering to the Tube or to get a cab, or on to the next place.

'Is tapas OK with you?' Ben asked.

There was a tapas bar in Bath but I'd never been in. 'Yeah, that'll be good.'

He led me along pathways and over a bridge that crossed one of the old docks, through darkening squares and past colonnades. Then, round a corner, I saw a bright neon sign: 'Tapas'. A delicious scent of garlic reached my nostrils, and I realised I was starving. Crisps are not enough supper for a growing girl.

We sat in a little booth, on black bench seats with high backs so no one could see you unless they walked right past. It was the kind of place I'd like to go on a date. I couldn't decide over the menu, so Ben ordered us a selection of tapas with names like *patatas bravas* and *gambas* (spicy potatoes and prawns, explained the menu). They arrived in small bowls and on dark red earthenware plates.

'I haven't been a very good mentor this evening, have I?' said Ben.

'What do you mean?'

'Oh, I don't know. Exposing you to hard-drinking journalists, plying you with alcohol when you're under age . . . That kind of thing.'

'At least you didn't offer me any coke,' I said, without thinking.

Ben looked startled. 'You noticed?'

'Of course! It wasn't exactly subtle. A Year Five kid

would have spotted something was going on. But I also noticed you didn't take any.'

'Yeah, well, we've got a big story to work on. And anyway I'm putting all that stuff behind me. It's not worth it, Becks, take it from me. It fucks with your head . . . But let's change the subject. Have I told you, you look amazing in that top?'

I grinned and nodded.

'Oh yeah, that's right – earlier today. And how about that I really like you, and think you'll make a great journalist?'

'No, you haven't told me that before.' There went one of those little jumps in my stomach and chest.

We talked and ate and talked some more. Ben told me about school in Bradford and uni at Exeter (he studied English). He told me about his mad flatmate and his mum and their dog back home. And how he didn't speak to his dad any more. We discussed politics and found we agreed on, like, practically everything. And we worked out solutions to world poverty and climate change and peace in the Middle East – if only people would listen to us.

And then Ben checked his watch and it was nearly one o'clock. No wonder I was starting to get sleepy.

He helped me on with my jacket, and we emerged into the night again. A black cab was passing in the street ahead of us, and Ben ran ahead to hail it.

'I'll come all the way with you and then go back to mine, so I can make sure you get in safely. I wouldn't want to be responsible for anything happening to you between the taxi and your front door.'

In the car, tired and happy, I relaxed against the big, upholstered seat and let myself lean in towards Ben. He didn't move away. He pulled me closer and I rested my head on his chest. I could hear his heart beating. Then I think he kissed my hair, but I'm not certain.

'Are you sure you're seventeen, Becky Dunford?'

'Mm. Yes.'

'Damn. Seventeen-year-olds are so much more grown-up these days. I'm sure I wasn't like you when I was your age.' He took my hand and stroked it gently with his fingers. 'You probably think I haven't noticed you. But I have. Well, not so much at first. But since we've been working together.'

I lifted my head and stroked his cheek. He didn't stop me. Ben hadn't shaved for a couple of days and his chin was rough with stubble.

'Oh no, this is such a bad idea, Becks. I'm a dangerous person to get involved with. And you're way too young. But I do really like you. You know that, don't you?'

I rested my head on his chest again and snuggled in close. 'What about Sarah and Alison?'

'That's what I mean,' he said. 'I think maybe they both like me – still like me – and I should be clear with them and stop it all. But I haven't. Sarah's a mate and a good friend, and I don't want to spoil that by saying anything. So you see I'm no good at all. I've let her go on liking me, and probably nothing will happen. Or maybe it will and then it'll be all messy, and awkward in the office, and people will get hurt . . .'

'And Alison?'

'Alison? Ah, Alison. Yes . . .' Ben held me tighter. 'It wouldn't work with Alison, I know it wouldn't . . . And as for you, you're better off without me. You should find a nice boy your own age.'

'There aren't any. I've looked,' I said into Ben's shirt. It smelled spicy and warm. Not of aftershave or too much deodorant. I don't like aftershave. It's too clean-cut.

The cab was near my dad's flat. I didn't want it to be. I wanted this journey to go on forever.

Ben did as he had said and saw me to my door. Was he going to kiss me?

'Do you want to come in?' I couldn't believe I was asking. And I didn't even know how much I wanted to happen. Just that ending the evening now would seem too cruel.

'No, Becks. Not a good idea. I'll see you tomorrow – get our Pulitzer prize-winning story published.'

He didn't kiss me. Not on the lips. He brushed his mouth against my cheek and then let go. 'Best get your key out,' he prompted.

'Night-night, Ben,' I said. I couldn't believe he was about to go.

'Look, Becks . . .' he said, from halfway between me and the taxi. 'It really wouldn't be a good idea. Trust me. Let's be friends, OK? Can we do that?'

In bed I replayed everything in the tapas restaurant and the cab, and then ran the movie-in-my-head on a bit further. I wondered what Ben's body was like under his clothes.

Then, just as I was drifting off happily, another thought barged into my mind. A thought about The Conversation.

If James Hepworth was such a hotshot PR and lobbyist, why would he have The Conversation on a train? I'd thought he was simply being stupid and arrogant, but surely he'd be cleverer than that. From what Dad had said about lobbyists, they knew the game inside out – they'd know to be ultra-discreet. So why hadn't Mr Pinstripe been more careful?

14

I was so glad I hadn't drunk. I felt a bit tired, but I'd soon recover. And anyway I was walking on air. Alison noticed when she came in with her coffee and dark circles under her eyes. 'How come you're looking so bouncy?' she asked. 'Some of us have hangovers to tend to. I must remember to go straight home tonight and cook myself something healthy and nutritious.'

'I only had orange juice,' I said. 'And lots of water later. And today we're going to see about getting the story into the paper.'

'We?'

'Ben. Me and Ben. He's probably talking to the editor now.'

'Oh. Right. I thought you meant your skincare one. But of course you've been working on that other story too. So it's going well?'

'Really well,' I said, and bounded off to my desk.

Ben had texted: Ed luvs it :o) bxx.

'Becky   ' It was Claire. She was on the phone and had her hand over the receiver as she talked to me. 'We're sorting out a photographer for your green cosmetics article. Can you go to Hansom & Divine this afternoon? The photographer can drive you. And if you could do the interview at the same time – it's the only slot they've both got free.'

'Yeah, that should be OK.' I was in the middle of texting Ben back.

How cool was that? The editor loved the article, which meant it might even go in tomorrow's paper!

There was a lot of messaging between me and Nita that morning, as I caught her up on the events of the night before. We arranged to go for lunch together and talk about it all some more.

I'd decided that wearing my other gorgeous (lucky?) top today would be too much. So it was back to my usual clothes. I had on a cute red T-shirt that I loved, even though it was from, like, more than a year ago. It had a retro design on the front, kind of 70s with a curly pattern, and the logo read: 'Ethics Girl'. I thought Ben would appreciate it. Mum had to explain about 'Essex Girls' to me, but the slogan's great anyway.

The weather was heading into another heatwave, and it was getting hot for jeans. I wondered whether I should buy a skirt or even a dress, but it would have to be cheap because my taxi money and my savings from working weekend shifts at Sainsbury's were running low (even though Ben paid for the cab last night). I might not be able to afford to stay in London, even if Mum and Dad let me.

Nita and I browsed through Topshop and Miss Selfridge

in the Canary Wharf mall. I munched on a veggie burger while she had some kind of minuscule salad. She was trying to get rid of her tummy, she said.

'What tummy? It's almost flat.'

'Yeah – *almost*. I need to lose a couple more centimetres and then it'll be absolutely and completely flat.'

She was wearing a shift dress with a black and white pattern that made your eyes go weird if you looked at it too long, and black patent pumps. She'd decided to go completely 60s and had spent the weekend raiding charity shops. My phone was full of pictures she'd sent me of her finds.

At last we found a skirt and some sandals that were on sale, and that we both agreed looked good on me.

And then Nita said something I didn't want to hear.

'Becky, I know you really like Ben, but you're not taking it seriously, are you? I'm sure he fancies you, but I don't know, I think maybe you could get hurt. I've heard things. It sounds like he's bad news . . .'

'Course I'm not taking it seriously,' I lied. 'He told me himself that it would be a bad idea to get involved with him. I'm just, you know, having fun. Enjoying myself in London.' Inside I was screaming: 'No, no, he's wonderful, I adore him. I want to be with him.'

'That's good, because I really think you should be careful. I didn't want to say before, this morning, because you've been so happy about everything. But Marty was saying about his last relationship . . . You know he thought Ben had been badly hurt and not recovered? Well, he found out that really what happened was Ben slept with someone else and that's why it all ended.'

My stomach dropped to my feet.

'And there's something else. I heard this woman talking in the toilets – she was at the basin and I was having a pee so she didn't see me. And she was saying about how Ben Hutchison had been stringing along this school kid wannabe journalist because he wanted to get her to spill some scandal about the government and her MP father, and how it was really disgusting and the lowest of the low to do something like that.'

My stomach dropped even further. That sounded more possible. But it was just this woman's opinion, and what if it was Sarah and she was being bitchy and spreading gossip about Ben? 'I'll be careful,' I said.

But what if I didn't feel like being careful?

'Hi, Becks, it's Ben. Look, do you want to come along to see James Hepworth with me? I'm leaving here at two. Give me a bell. Bye.'

Ben must have called while I was trying stuff on in Topshop. I'd thought he was going to meet Mr Pinstripe on his own – not freak him out by a schoolgirl journalist tagging along. But I couldn't miss this opportunity, could I?

Shit. I'd forgotten about the other interview I was supposed to be doing. The one with Hansom & Divine. If I was going to catch Ben I needed to leave pretty much right away. Maybe they could reschedule.

Claire wasn't at her desk. Agitated, I asked Tallulah if she knew where she was. 'Gone to lunch,' she said. 'Something I can help with?'

'No, yes, no. Thanks but no. I'll leave her a note.'

Dear Claire,

Sorry, but I won't be able to make the interview this afternoon, as I have to go out for another important meeting for the paper (back by 4.30 p.m.). Would it be possible to do it tomorrow instead? I'm very sorry about the short notice, but I've only just heard about this.
Becky

I'd remembered from before to let Claire know what I was doing, and when to expect me back (I learn fast, me). I hoped it would be all right. I hoped she could read my writing. And I hoped I wouldn't be causing too much trouble.

I rushed past Nita and garbled a mixed-up message about where I was going while I tried to ring Ben at the same time. Dictaphone, better take my dictaphone. Although Ben would have one, wouldn't he? Better take it anyway. And check I had my notebook. And a pen.

Of course James Hepworth wasn't meeting us at his office. Why had I thought he would? I'd imagined walking into another huge building with a huge atrium – a bit like 1 Canada Square, but with a different colour scheme – and being zoomed up in a lift (perhaps one of those glass ones that glide up the outside of buildings) to his executive office. But no. We were in a gloomy café that sold falafels and filled pittas and greasy-looking aubergine and tomato stew.

'Actually, the food's pretty good here,' Mr Pinstripe said smoothly (except he wasn't wearing a pinstripe today). He must have noticed my disparaging look. 'Have we met before?'

He held out his hand to shake mine.

'Erm, kind of.'

'Becky's the one who got you on tape. Or audio file, to be more exact. In fact, I thought maybe I could play you what she recorded, and you could fill in some gaps for us. How does that sound?'

Mr Non-Pinstripe smirked. 'Really. Like I'm going to do that for you. Hand you everything on a plate.'

'So why've you agreed to this meeting, then? I was expecting to hear from Auricle's lawyers, not get a face-to-face.'

I sat quietly, watching as the two professionals circled one another.

James Hepworth took a long slurp of dark brown tea. Then he put down the thick china cup. There was a puddle of tea in the saucer. It was strange: here he was, Mr Pinstripe, The Conversation man, sitting across a laminate-topped table from me.

'I wouldn't normally be stupid enough to let my business be heard on a train . . .' (So I'd been right about that.) 'But I had my reasons on this occasion – and it seems to have worked. And I have my reasons for seeing you now.'

'And they are . . .?' said Ben.

James wasn't going to be hurried. He chased a piece of cucumber round his plate with his fork. 'Why do you think I went into lobbying? And no, it wasn't for the money. Although that comes in handy. I'd been an MP's researcher, but my MP didn't do as well as I'd been hoping, and when there was nowhere to go at Westminster except down or sideways, I skipped out. But I wanted to keep close to the action.'

'Come on, cut to the chase.' Ben was drumming his fingers on the table. As I watched his hands I remembered them running through my hair in the cab.

James put down his fork and stared Ben straight in the eye. 'You need to know this to understand why I'm seeing you, and why I'm going to tell you what I am. OK?'

'OK, all right. No need to kick off.'

'So . . . What you've found so far is correct. But it goes deeper than that. The whole gold trade is very complicated. Some gold comes from new, mined sources. Some of it is from scrap that's been melted down. Jewellers buy it from banks, and from refiners like us, but by that time, generally, the chain linking back to its original source is almost impossible to trace. The point of this being' – James Hepworth wiped his mouth on a thin paper napkin – 'that in the past we didn't know exactly where our gold came from. And, quite frankly, as long as the price was right, we wouldn't care.'

'So how come you knew that this gold – that you've sold to Lina and I guess other places too – was dirty gold, or conflict gold even?' I couldn't resist asking the question that was burning in my head.

'Because, young lady, we had a tip-off. We were offered some gold that at face value looked as though it had a clean bill of health. But then we were told that it was almost certainly from the DRC – that's the Democratic Republic of Congo – and had been smuggled into Uganda.'

'So you were being misled and you found out about it – why didn't you just report it?'

'Ah, well. That's where it all starts to look worse for Auricle. We could have, and even requested an investigation, but instead we decided to turn a blind eye. We didn't want to lose our custom to a competitor. When it came down to it we had an order to fill and not enough gold to fill it – not without this new gold anyway.'

'But why . . . ?' I asked. 'Especially if Auricle was setting itself up as being more ethical?'

'It's business, isn't it? Supply and demand. And anyway we had assurances that made it appear less of a risk.' James paused for another mouthful of tea. 'Let's say there was support from certain places that made it seem like something we wouldn't have to worry about.'

I hadn't a clue what he meant, but it sounded as though this was starting to get to the kernel of what had gone on. Gradually we were peeling back the layers.

'What kind of involvement?' Ben asked.

'Official,' said James. 'Well, not exactly official but a person who's close to government. In fact, the person who gave us the tip-off.'

'So why didn't he go public about it?' I asked.

'Oh, no, he's not going to be blowing any whistles on us . . .' James looked upwards, examining the yellowing flakes of paint on the ceiling. 'Auricle donates a lot of money to the Party, you see. No point him upsetting the company directors for no reason. The government could do without any more scandals about its donors. And of course Auricle doesn't want even a hint of this to get out either – just think what would happen to our sales if it did.'

'But it has to get out!' I cried, almost jumping out of my chair.

'Exactly. Which is why I decided to talk to you.'

Ben had his head down, turning over a teaspoon in his hands. He looked unfazed by what we'd just been told. 'So what kind of support was this government person offering? Was he getting something personally out of it too, as well as saving face for the Party? And who is it anyway?'

'I've told you everything I can. You'll have to find out the rest on your own. At the moment it can look like a PR cock-up – me not being on top of my job and letting some inopportune words slip, coupled with two journalists putting two and two together. I'll have a chance to resign and hopefully that will be it. The rest will come out in time. But if I give you any more, then he'll know it's me and he'll come after me, and deny everything I've told you, and it could all get very unpleasant.'

James Hepworth picked up his briefcase and jacket and motioned over to the woman behind the counter to bring his bill.

'So why do we need to understand why you went into lobbying?' Ben asked. 'I'm not quite clear on that one.'

'Because I started out wanting to change the world – probably a bit like Becky here – and wanting to be an MP,' said James as he counted coins on to a saucer that held the bill. 'I ate, slept, dreamed politics and the political world. I helped this lot win the last election. But I've done so much lying and spinning in my time and now I've had it with all that. This is one I can't stomach. It's gone too far.'

'You won't have a job if we print this . . .' I said quietly.

'No. And I don't want one. I'm going to Australia, to start a new life with my girlfriend out there. Do something completely different – though don't expect me to send you a postcard.'

He glanced at the door. 'Look, I need to be gone now. I'm asking that you don't quote me – keep everything off the record – as a favour in return for the one I've done you. Use any of what I've given you today, by all means, and the phone call on the train, but nothing to suggest I've actually spoken to you, OK? Keep it all speculation. I'm not that nice a person that I'll let you get away with naming me.'

The words from the recording echoed through my head again: 'No, no, no. They must not find out. We can't let that happen. OK? Do what you have to . . .'

Perhaps their meaning hadn't been as sinister as I'd imagined. Perhaps, even, the note of drama had been designed to catch the attention of someone like me. But I still figured that James Hepworth wasn't a man I wanted to mess with.

As our informant closed the café door behind him, Ben turned to me: 'You get all that?'

'I hope so,' I said, pressing the 'Stop' button on my shiny little dictaphone.

'How could you do that? Couldn't they rearrange the interview for another time? I could've done it all on the phone tomorrow or Friday. There was no need . . .'

I was pissed off with Nita and I had every right to be. She'd only gone and nicked my story. I knew she was ambitious, but I didn't think she'd go behind my back and steal my interview, the cow. And I thought we were friends.

What else was she being less than straight up with me about? Perhaps she was in the 'I fancy Ben' queue too, and was trying to get rid of the competition by telling tales about him to me . . .

'Claire said it was the only time they could do the interview together,' Nita said. She was doing fake-concerned really well. 'She thought it was better to do it now rather than risk them not being available. They're going to Japan, or one of them is, so they wouldn't be around another time. I thought you'd be OK about it. Really. I'm sorry.'

Claire appeared at my shoulder. 'Something the matter?'

'Yes. Why'd you say Nita could do my interview?'

'Well, you weren't here, and it was short notice, and I thought we should get some words to go on the page, since we were sending a photographer along. I don't think you can really get huffy about it, given that you were off somewhere else. It's not that big a deal, anyway. This is only part of the piece. Surely you two can come to some arrangement about a shared byline?'

I went home to Dad's flat without saying goodbye to Nita. Childish, I know, but I wanted both of my stories – 'dirty' gold and 'clean' cosmetics – to have my name on them. Maybe I wanted too much. Maybe I was spoiled. But it didn't stop me wanting.

15

Part of my blog entry for Thursday 31 July:

i'm gonna have to write this in my blog
because i don't think it's ever going to
appear in the paper. i'm gutted and i
really don't understand why it's happened.
one minute the editor luvs this story the
next he says he isn't interested! he said
it wudn't stand up cos we only have the
word of someone who won't be quoted. it's
like he's had a complete turnaround over
it. why???? i can't figure it out. unless
someone is putting pressure on the ed not
to publish.

dad has told me about how mean n dirty
things can get in politics. you know the
party whips - they're like the enforcers -
they make mps vote the way they want them
to. it's the same with all the parties. if

there's anything dodgy in ur past whether it's an affair or tax evasion or anything like that then they make it their business to know about it and they'll threaten to go public if u don't vote the way they want. so maybe this govt person mr pinstripe talked about has that kind of info about the ed??

i am so depressed about this and also what if ben has really just been using me? i don't believe it tho. how cud he make up the stuff in the tapas restaurant or the cab? but it made me not want to go into the office today. i think maybe i'll go home to bath tomorrow after all. i can do my last interview with mum's spa people in the afternoon and then write up the article over the weekend.

i'll keep you up to date if anything more happens with the dirty gold story.

Ben had been emailing me all morning, saying not to lose heart. If we found this government official person, and uncovered the rest of what had been going on, then that should be enough to make the editor 'interested' and print our story. Ben had already rung Auricle, when we got back yesterday, to ask for an interview with one of the top bods. They'd refused of course, and when he confronted them with our findings they said – predictably – 'No comment', and then issued a bland statement about how everyone was working together to ensure sustainability and ethical practices in mining and jewellery. Blah blah – it was all fake; they didn't really care, did they? And they certainly weren't going to come clean without being forced to.

I felt I had to do something – so that's why I started blogging about it. I hadn't been going to write about The Conversation in my blog, but I wanted the story told – even if I wasn't going to get my name on the front page of the *Courier*. So I dashed off a few words in my spare moments at *Sunday Style*.

Suddenly I was feeling very far away from everything and everyone I knew. I wanted Sally to be with me. I missed her, and her sense of humour and good advice. She'd get me to laugh off my dark mood. I wasn't completely avoiding Nita, but I felt more cautious. Was she really someone I could trust? She was going around looking sheepish and texting and messaging to say how sorry she was, and how she hadn't meant to upset me. She wanted us to go out with some friends of hers in the evening, but I wasn't in the mood.

I sat doodling all over a page of my notebook. Scrawly flowers and scratchy black squares. I was supposed to be taking notes from Claire about writing up my 'green' cosmetics article. But I was struggling to listen. It was like at school, when you know the teacher's saying something you should be concentrating on, but somehow your mind won't stay still. It keeps drifting off on to something else, and instead of writing words your pen is scribbling nonsense and pictures.

Alison had told me a great journalist's trick for if you haven't been listening to someone properly, or haven't been taking notes. At the end you say to them: 'Could you email all that to me?'

Claire was speaking. 'I'll be around of course to look over it with you, so make sure you give me a section as soon as you've written it.' She paused. 'You think you'll be OK writing this article?'

'Mm, yes. But it would be great to have your notes so I can look at them at home. Do you think you could email them to me?'

'No problem,' Claire replied, glancing at my notepad. I couldn't really try to hide it with my hand like a young kid would. Claire opened her mouth to say something, then closed it again and swivelled back to her computer screen. After a few minutes her email came through. 'Is there something the matter?' she'd typed at the end.

'Thank you but I'm OK,' I emailed back. Claire smiled over, then dashed off to do some important Beauty business.

That morning I was quite happy to do undemanding tasks, like sitting and sorting Claire's mail, and organising product samples for the *Sunday Style* expert tester to review. It meant I didn't have to think. In the afternoon I'd have to get on with my cosmetics article and do some interviews over the phone.

It's hard trying to type when you've got a phone wedged between your ear and your shoulder and you aren't very good at typing anyway. So Ben had lent me this special earpiece that records while you speak. It's like a one-sided iPod headphone. I was looking forward to trying it out. It made me feel almost like a spy. Claire said you had to let people know when you were recording them, but Ben clearly didn't feel that was necessary. Not if our meeting with James Hepworth was anything to go by.

Ben had been given another story to work on for the next day's paper, so he was too busy to follow up on James Hepworth's government official (and he couldn't meet me for lunch, he texted, apologising). I couldn't risk taking any more time away from my *Sunday Style* stuff to chase leads either – if I wasn't careful, before I knew it my cosmetics article would have Nita's name all over it instead of mine.

I just wanted to be home – London home, in Dad's flat. Able to mope about by myself, and watch rubbish TV and eat something crappy and heated up in the oven. A Dad special. Jake emailed and offered to come over when I got back from work, but I wasn't even in the mood for Jake. Which is extremely unusual. He'd taken me to the cinema the previous night, to go and see what he said was a 'classic Hong Kong martial arts movie' at the National Film Theatre. It was OK, but not quite my thing. Then we went to a noodle bar in Chinatown – because Jake said it was the cheapest thing he could think of to eat, apart from McDonald's – and he gave me a lecture about 'what (some) men are like', saying that in his opinion, I should forget all about Ben.

The hours dragged by. At lunchtime I kept my head bent so Nita wouldn't come and want to be all friendly and for us to go out together. Long hair is useful sometimes; with my head low no one could exactly see my face. If I could've got away with wearing shades indoors I would've today. There was this old Hollywood star (I mean, like, really old, from the 1930s) called Greta Garbo who was renowned for being a recluse. She was Swedish and her catchphrase was: 'I want to be alone.' I read that in a movie history book.

Two o'clock, time for my first interview. I got myself ready and checked my dictaphone and did a test on the microphone with Alison. 'Hello, is that Miss Becky Dunford?' she said, in a posh accent. 'I'm the wife of a leading Tory MP and I'd like to tell you all about my husband's scandalous affairs. How much do you think you can pay me?'

We laughed. And the microphone worked too. It was the most fun I'd had all day.

In the end the interview went fine, and I transcribed the audio file straight away, just like Claire's instructions suggested. I had another interview later on, and that was OK too. By the end of the afternoon I could have gone on *Mastermind* with 'Green cosmetics, and the chemicals we maybe shouldn't be putting on our skin' as my chosen subject. I even knew what parabens were. (They're chemicals used as a preservative in stuff like shampoo and deodorants. People have been worried about links with breast cancer since a study published in 2004 found parabens in breast tumours. Some people also get an allergic reaction. The cosmetics industry and other studies say they're safe – but what if there's something they've missed? Maybe it's a good thing Mum's been bringing home all those samples from the spa.)

I was so glad when it was time to leave the office. Even though I was starting to get into researching my cosmetics story, I couldn't keep thoughts about The Conversation and Ben and Sarah and Nita from finding their way into my consciousness. In the supermarket I joined the queue of Canary Wharf commuters buying their supper. 'Cashier number five, please.' I paid for my ready meal and headed for the Tube.

At Oval I got the keys to Dad's flat ready. I liked to have them in my hand as I walked along. Afterwards my palm smelled of metal.

The flat was on the first floor and had a small roof terrace. I took a chair to sit outside and make some phone calls. The leaves on the neighbouring trees looked dark and sticky. You could tell out here that it was the end of a long, hot day in London, but for most of the time I'd been in the 'other world' of the tower at 1 Canada Square, insulated from the real temperature by air-conditioning.

I tried calling Sally, but she didn't answer, so I rang Jake. He offered again to come over, and I thought about it but decided no (again). And then he mentioned that Sharpedge were playing this weekend and Rich had specifically asked him to invite me. 'And what about Nita?' Jake added. 'Do you think she'd like to come?' I explained why Nita wasn't my favourite person right now. Jake said maybe I shouldn't be too harsh or too hasty. There was a chance she could be right about Ben, and that she hadn't really meant to steal my story. I huffed. I kind of knew in my head I wouldn't hold it against her for long, but I wasn't ready to make up yet.

I didn't feel hungry, so I got out Dad's old computer and began aimlessly searching around. And then it became more focused: there must be a way of at least narrowing down who this government official might be. I couldn't be sure whether James Hepworth had meant an MP, an adviser, or a civil servant. Which department might know about dirty gold trafficking? I started trawling round the .gov.uk sites, looking at lists of names and job titles and remits. With the Congo link it could be the Foreign Office, or else perhaps the Department of Trade and Industry. Or perhaps it was even something to do with one of the committees, like Dad's Environmental Audit Committee.

Dad! Perhaps I should ask him. I mean, he wouldn't know exactly who it was, but he could have a guess based on what James Hepworth had said.

I rang home. Mum answered and asked how the cosmetics story was going and which train was I getting home this weekend. I said fine, and maybe I might come back tomorrow and go to the spa for the interview instead of doing it on the phone, and she said, 'That's great. It's strange here without you. I miss you being here.'

Mum was being especially sweet – what was going on? I wondered for a moment if I missed home too. But right now it seemed that there was too much going on here in London to have any time for homesickness.

'Is Dad around?' I asked.

'He's just here. I'll pass you over. See you tomorrow then, sweetie. Lots of love.'

I explained to Dad about the story, as far as I felt I could (not mentioning James Hepworth by name – a journalist has to protect their sources). I could hear him getting off the sofa and creaking up the stairs to his study.

'It's a difficult one for me, Becks. You know I'd love to help. And it sounds like something that needs exposing. But it could put me in a difficult position. I can't be seen to be leaking information to the press.'

'Oh.'

'Look, leave it with me. If there's something in the public domain, that you could have found yourself, then that might be easier. Or I suppose you are one of my constituents, so I could always call it "a query from a concerned constituent"!' he joked.

'Thanks, Dad, that would be brilliant.'

'I can't promise anything though.' He paused. 'Becks – I'm really proud of you, you know.'

After that I started to feel less depressed about everything. Maybe we would nail this story after all, and unmask the villains. I thought I'd call Ben and tell him. I picked up my phone to search for his number. Then I put it down again. We hadn't really talked properly since the other night. I mean, it'd been under the surface – plenty of looks and smiles, and on our visit to see James Hepworth he'd kept kind of brushing against me or touching my hand when he didn't need to. OK so he'd warned me off, but he wasn't exactly backing away, and it had just made me more intrigued – more hooked. I realised that I really, really wanted him.

I picked up my phone once more and this time I rang him. 'Ben H,' said my mobile display.

'Hi, Becks,' said Ben's voice.

'Hi,' I replied.

'What're you up to?'

'I'm at my dad's. Thought I'd have a night in.' ('Why don't you come over?' was what I wanted to say. But I didn't. It wouldn't be cool. What if he said no and gave me all that stuff again about why nothing was going to happen?) 'I've been talking to my dad about whether he might have any ideas about the government official.'

'Strange you should say that, because I've just given our friend James Hepworth a call – see if I could get any more out of him. Of course, he was very cagey, almost refused to speak to me. But then he did say that there's some super-VIP function on tomorrow night. The CEO and some other people from Auricle will be there, and also some government bods. He wouldn't say if they included our man, but he did

140

hint very strongly it could be advantageous to our story if we were able to go along.'

'That's great!' I said, already planning how I was going to tell Mum I wasn't coming home tomorrow after all.

Ben added, 'Now I just need to work out how we can get an invite.'

16

My blog entry for Friday 1 August:

if u wanna find out more about dirty gold
then u cud check out this article from the
independent and another good one from the
guardian. it's really upsetting thinking
that children cud be breathing in mercury
fumes as they extract tiny amounts of gold
in their own homes. it puts u off ever
wearing gold again unless it's from
somewhere you absolutely know is ethical
or it's from hundreds of years ago.

anyway 2nite i am hoping to find out more
n maybe even unmask the b@*?@!*! our
contact talked about who has been covering
things up - or worse.

check here 2morrow to see what i've found
out. u can look at yesterday's post for

more about the story so far.

That morning I was too busy to worry about whether I was speaking to Nita or not. I had to make sure my last interviews for the green cosmetics article were all sorted. I had to let the spa know that I wouldn't be coming after all in person and make sure that Debbie and Carol, who I needed to speak to, would be around this afternoon and available by phone. I had to put together the products to be sent by courier to Susie Fay's studio. Then there was Claire's post, and some other errands for her, and a coffee run. Oh yeah, and I had to ring my mum. (I didn't feel like it last night. I was on too much of a high after Ben's phone call and I didn't want her bursting my bubble.)

I thought Mum was going to go mental and we'd have one of our arguments. But she was OK. I almost tried to pick a fight with her anyway, just so it would follow the normal pattern. But she wouldn't go for it. Maybe it was having Matt home. He's always been her favourite, did I tell you that? Oh yeah, I did . . . It's like, she's always trying to run my life, but she kind of basks in his – the constant proud parent. Even after he missed the A-level grades he needed for his first choices, and only just scraped a uni place through clearing. When he was made captain of the uni rugby second team it was like he couldn't do anything wrong, ever again. (My mum has always loved rugby, or so she says; Dad tolerates it; I only go to see Matt play when it's a family three-line whip or I'm feeling particularly sisterly and prepared to sit out the boredom.)

By lunchtime it was all sorted and I was feeling just a bit smug. This journalism business wasn't so difficult after all. I'd sooner do this than differentiation or the laws of motion any day. I couldn't believe how nervous I'd been about calling people when I first started, compared with now. I mean, I still had to take a breath before I picked up the phone – I'm not so much of a confident motormouth I can spew it out like some people – but after a few calls it became, like – you're only talking to another human being.

'Hi, it's Ben.'

'I know,' I said into my phone as I headed out towards the lift.

'I think I have a cunning plan for tonight. But you're going to need a party frock and I've been calling around to hire a dinner jacket. We can't get in as ourselves, so we're going to be Mr and Mrs Beaumont-Dillon.'

'Beaumont-What? They sound like they'd be about a hundred. Won't somebody notice?' My stomach did a trampoline jump as the lift bounced to a halt at the ground floor. I was going to be married to Ben – for one night only.

We huddled around a table at the Costa coffee shop, planning our strategy. Our heads were so close I could almost brush against Ben's stubble. I ran my hand oh-so-gently but casually over his chin: 'That'll have to go before tonight, then,' I said, with a cheeky look.

He rubbed at his several-days' growth. 'You think so? Yeah, maybe it doesn't quite fit the profile.'

Ben had managed to wangle the tickets through someone he was at uni with who knew someone else who knew someone who felt they weren't well enough paid for the job they were doing at the rather large company that was organising the event, and was happy to pass on an invite in the name of someone who'd just RSVP'd to say they weren't going. Especially if there were some nice bottles of wine as a reward.

'But that's bribery!' I said. 'Isn't that against the journalist's code of ethics?'

'What code of ethics?' replied Ben. 'I thought everyone believed journalists don't have any kind of morality anyway. And it's in a good cause, isn't it? What harm are we doing? Absolutely none.'

I wasn't so sure. But I didn't have time to come up with a convincing argument. Plus I was too excited about going to the party, and what might happen. The big question was – what on earth was I going to wear?

It was lucky that Nita and I had made up. Really, I was being a bitch before, wasn't I? Putting her down like that and believing the worst of her. It's not like me normally. When I came into the office this morning I wasn't bothered whether we spoke to each other or not. But by the afternoon I was gagging to talk to someone else about the party, and Jake and Sally were both otherwise occupied and not answering my texts. (Sally had her phone switched off – maybe she was taking some poor house-hunters round an overpriced shack;

or maybe she'd sneaked away somewhere with Steve.)

I still thought Nita was wrong about Ben, but she'd been very sweet about the green article and said she didn't need to have her name on it at all, it could just be mine. So of course I said that she could have a byline too, on the part that she's done. It was only fair.

So once that was all cleared up, I could stop feeling bad about it and trying to avoid Nita's eye.

Her face lit up when I told her about my party-wear problem. It's exactly her idea of heaven: a glamorous makeover. I told her she had her work cut out and she said, 'Nonsense.' I don't know, I've never been so self-conscious about the way I look as I have since I started here. It's not that everyone in the office looks like Keira Knightley. They really don't (although Claire is gorgeous). But reading *Sunday Style*, and the other magazines around the office, I've become so aware of all the things I don't do, and my skin, and my figure, and all the make-up and clothes I should have in order to be fashionable . . . I'm a low-maintenance kind of girl, but I feel as though I ought to be high-maintenance, you know?

'It'll be our own private dressing-up cupboard,' said Nita, as we walked back with the afternoon's coffee and tea supplies (and biscuits and chocolate) from the canteen.

'What? The fashion cupboard?' I replied. 'But there'll be people here still. We can't just disappear behind the door while Claire and Tallulah and everyone sit there wondering what the hell we're doing.' I thought for a moment. 'What if we tell people the truth?'

Nita gave me a look that said: 'Are you completely off your trolley?'

'Well – a version of the truth. Say I've got some party to go to with my dad – like the last one, but posher . . . No?'

I thought it could work. But Nita had a much more ambitious vision for my attire.

'The kind of dress I have in mind, Becky, they're not going to let you out of the office in it, let alone to a party where there might be wine and finger food that could ruin it.'

'Oh. OK. So what's your idea?'

'You can come to my house. My mum won't mind. She'll probably help with your hair. I need to make a few calls, then I'll let you know what we have.'

Nita walked with elegant, purposeful steps round to her desk. She handed out her spoils then said something to Tallulah, who nodded. Nita opened Tallulah's drawer and took out her prized Contacts Book – the Fashion editor's special scrapbook of names and collections and, importantly, phone numbers. Marty, Tallulah's assistant, gave Nita an eyebrows-raised stare, but then Nita whispered to him, he glanced over at me, smiled, nodded, waved, nodded at Nita and then let her carry on. Phew. Not sure what she said, but we were on course.

Then I had to do my interview with Debbie and Carol at the spa. I've met them before, so it was all quite easy. But I couldn't concentrate on writing it up. I'd have to do all that over the weekend now.

147

Instead I had a quick look through the beauty samples to see if there was anything that might come in handy. I picked out a few tubes that promised dewy skin and party glow and leafed through copies of *Vogue* to see what sophisticated make-up they suggested. I slipped a couple of issues into my bag. No one would miss them. And how was I going to make my hair look anything special? I messaged Nita and she told me not to worry about any of it.

Ben texted to say that he'd picked up his suit and the invite. Only six hours to go till party time, and the birth of Becky Dunford, undercover journalist.

17

'Thanks, I'm fine. It's delicious, I just can't eat any more,' I said, as Mrs Mistry hovered over my plate.

'Not if she's going to fit into her dress,' added Nita.

Almost as soon as I came in through the door Nita's mum had wanted to feed me. She kept asking what I liked to eat, and would I like to try this or that. Her food was really good. And all veggie too, which suited me.

'But you eat prawns at the office . . .' I said to Nita, when her mother was explaining about being vegetarian because they were Gujarati Hindus.

'Sshh! She doesn't know. It's the one thing I'm bad about. I never eat beef, or even chicken, and not even eggs most of the time. Only prawns and mayo. That's it.' She shouted across to her mother in the kitchen: 'Mum, can you help with Becky's hair? I've got a photo from a magazine . . .'

Nita handed the picture to her mother, and then she and I climbed up the wide, carpeted stairs to an attic room. 'This is mine,' said Nita. 'What do you think?'

The room held at least four clothes rails, filled with what looked like everything Nita must have worn since the age of thirteen. The rails were the main feature as you walked in, making it look like backstage at a fashion show. Beyond them were mannequin heads with wigs, and a sewing machine, and pictures from magazines papering the walls with fashions of every kind you could imagine. Under her bed were more stacks of magazines. And piled on top of it were the zippered clothes bags that Nita had redirected from *Sunday Style* to her parents' house.

'Nita! The room's fantastic . . . And you got all this past Tallulah?' I said, impressed, heading over towards the treasures on the bed.

'Tallulah wasn't a problem, she doesn't really keep a track of things, as you may have noticed. Marty said he'd cover for me unless anything gets damaged – he got all excited when I told him about you going undercover. And anyway, I'm only borrowing them – we'll send it all back tomorrow.'

Nita stroked her hand proudly over the bags.

'I told the designers I was calling the dresses in for a shoot for the magazine, but Marty says he'll tell them it had to be cancelled. The problem will be if Poppy' – Jan's PA – 'starts asking about the address on the courier dockets, and why the clothes were sent here instead of the office or a photographer's studio.'

She turned to me. 'You ready for this?'

Nita unzipped each bag in turn and streams of silk and chiffon and eye-popping reds and clear whites and jewel colours and stylish neutrals cascaded on to Nita's duvet. I hardly dared to touch them. They rustled out of the bags –

'Oh, a Chloé!' I couldn't help gasping. (I may not be a fashionaholic, but I do know some labels.)

'I don't want you to look at the names,' said Nita. 'I want you to try them on without knowing the designer, so you'll be persuaded by what looks good on you, not who made it.'

'OK,' I agreed meekly, happy to put myself in Nita's hands. If I trusted anyone's style, it was hers.

I kind of lost count, with trying on one thing and then another again, and then on to something else, but there must have been about ten dresses, and six pairs of shoes, from spindly stilettos to high-rise wedges. Mum had insisted on watching a silly film once about a female agent who went undercover. *Modesty Blaise*, it was called. Anyway, she was wearing a different outfit in every scene. I felt a bit like that.

Nita would be nodding or shaking her head almost before I'd smoothed each dress down. She stood behind and inspected me in the mirror.

'That one's lovely,' she said of a pale blue, boho-style dress, 'but you still look seventeen. You need something that's going to make people think you're at least twenty.'

I was posing in a black and white dress that I imagined someone like Nicole Kidman wearing when my phone buzzed from my bag. (I'd got into the same habit as everyone in the office, of putting it on to 'vibrate'.)

'That's the one,' said Nita, as I tried to walk delicately over (despite my heels) to answer it. Must be Ben, to tell me the venue – at last. He kept refusing to let me know where we were going. 'It'll be more of a surprise,' he had teased. It was probably going to be some boring stuffy embassy place anyway.

'Dad?' That wasn't the name I'd been expecting to show on the screen.

'Hi, Becks, are you somewhere you can talk for a moment?'

'Yes . . .' What was this about?

'I've made a few enquiries, seeing what I could find out about this story of yours . . . Thing is, Becks, I'd like you to . . . I'm asking you to stop.'

'What?'

'Stop writing the story. Don't get any further into all this business. It's not a good idea.'

'But I thought you were on my side! Are you trying to say I shouldn't tell the truth, or try to find it out? What's happened? Why are you doing this?' I couldn't believe this from my dad. From him of all people.

'I've spoken to the editor of the *Courier*—'

'You spoke to the editor!'

'Yes, Rebecca, I did.' It was a bad sign when Dad used my full name. 'I wanted to check his view on this story. And he agrees with me. It's not worth the trouble it would cause.'

'But I thought the editor just wasn't interested in the story – that's what he told Ben, anyway. Now you're saying someone's going to cause trouble for us all if we go on with it?' Something wasn't right here. This wasn't like my dad.

'Well, no, not exactly. What I mean is . . . Becky, please just do what I ask you, OK? I'm sure it'll all come out in the end. But not now – and not through this investigation you're doing with – erm – Ben Hutchison.'

'Hmm.' I wasn't convinced, so I made a sort of grumpy harrumphing noise. I was disappointed. Why was Dad being so lame about this? Couldn't we just take on whoever was obviously putting pressure on him and the editor, and expose what they were doing?

'I can't really explain why I'm asking you to stop, and I don't want to insult your intelligence by making something up,' Dad continued, sounding weary. 'But there are some things – about my work and what's been happening lately – that it's just better if you don't know the full details of, all right?'

'So you're telling me to forget about all of this?' I said, half angry and half deflated. 'But what happens if the story doesn't come out? I can't believe you're doing this, Dad. It's so unlike you. And it's so unfair. This is my story, and it's important, and I want it to be printed, not get swept under the carpet and forgotten about.'

'I know, Becks. I'm sorry. But I'm afraid that's the way it's got to be. OK?'

'I don't know, Dad . . .' In the background I could hear, faintly, an announcement: 'The train is now approaching London Paddington, our final station stop . . .' 'Dad, are you in London?'

'Oh – yes. I have to meet with some colleagues. I

might stay at the flat tonight, so I'll see you later, maybe.' He paused. 'Becks – promise you won't do any more . . . Whatever you're thinking of doing, please don't do it.'

'I don't think I can do that, Dad.' And before he had a chance to say anything else, I added, 'I'll call you and Mum tomorrow. I'm going out with Nita tonight, I might stay over at her house.' And then I clicked my phone shut.

Of course I wasn't going out with Nita, but it might be an idea to stay with her tonight anyway. Especially as I had no intention of giving up on this story. I was so disappointed in my dad, and confused as to why he was behaving like this. If I hadn't been on such a high about the party I might have slumped down right there and got all mardy about it. But my stylist was waiting for me . . .

Nita had been considerately busying herself with setting up her make-up table. She'd laid everything out neatly in front of a professional-style mirror with bulbs all round the edge.

'Are you all right, Becky? I couldn't help hearing . . .'

I nodded. 'I'm OK. Thanks.' I went over and gave Nita a hug. 'I'm glad you're here. And I'm sorry again. About before.'

'No problem. But perhaps you could give some warning next time you plan to throw a hissy-fit at me.' We both smiled. 'Now – eyebrows first.'

I climbed out of the precious dress and Nita and her mother began attending to my beauty needs, working together and around each other. This must be how it felt to be a pampered celeb. I sat and did what I was told (mainly keeping still and not talking too much), as my eyebrows were tweezered into shape, my nails (hands and feet) were softened, trimmed and lacquered, and my hair was expertly teased and pinned and sprayed and groomed. Nita's mum had given me a sleek 'up' style that definitely made me look older. Then it was time for the make-up.

'You'll have lovely skin when the acne stops,' teased Nita.

'Geez, thanks,' I replied, swatting her. Nita giggled.

'Don't worry, my bag of tricks will fix it,' she said.

By the time she'd finished I hardly recognised myself. But in a good way.

'What do you think?' she asked.

'It's fantastic. Thank you. I could never've done this myself. I wouldn't have a clue where to start.'

I kept catching glimpses of myself in the mirror as I changed into my party clothes. What would Ben think? My heart raced. No, Becky – you're supposed to be doing a job here, being the principled investigative journalist chasing down a crook and revealing a story that the public has a right to know about . . . Yeah, but if I had a good time too, that wouldn't be a sin, would it . . .?

The doorbell rang.

I practised walking elegantly down the stairs, and hoped my ankle wouldn't let me down like it had at the Houses of Parliament.

Nita had opened the door and Ben was on the doorstep, in a formal black suit, white shirt and black bow-tie.

'You look like you should be on *Strictly Come Dancing*,' I said.

'And you look . . . fabulous,' he replied. 'My jaw is

officially on the floor. You look amazing, Becky. Every man there will be jealous.'

I felt myself blushing. I hoped it wouldn't show too much.

We were stuck in a cab on the North Circular. Not so glamorous. 'So it can't be anywhere in central London,' I said. 'Or this would be a very funny way to get there.'

We inched along. The cab had a whiff of burgers. I was glad Nita had made me wear perfume – I didn't want to arrive smelling like a McDonald's. 'Spray it in the air and walk through it,' she'd instructed me. 'That's the way to make sure you're wearing exactly the right amount.' I was such a first-grader when it came to all this beauty stuff.

Ben checked his watch. 'We're still OK for time. As long as we're there in half an hour or so.'

We sat in the traffic some more, our conversation as stationary as the car. I'd thought we'd be gabbling away, but I reckon Ben was genuinely nervous, and it held me back from jabbering on. I pulled a folded sheet of paper out of my bag. On it were printed a set of photos: these were the people we were going to be on the lookout for, and spying on.

What we wanted to spot was any of them talking to someone Ben might recognise as being in any way related to the government. Ideally all of them in a gaggle, perhaps heading off to some private room for a secret gathering. I know – that was a bit unlikely. But we could always hope.

'Wembley!' I saw a sign for the turn-off that was coming up and it clicked. 'That's where we're going, isn't it?'

'Yep, you've guessed it. Happy now?' Ben looked pleased with himself.

'I can't believe it. That's amazing. This has made my whole year, practically. I've never been. I mean, Dad keeps saying he'll try to get us in, but he's never managed to . . . Wembley!' I couldn't resist it – I gave Ben a kiss. On the cheek though. I didn't want to appear too forward.

And maybe I was nervous too. Not so much about the story – somehow I felt that would all fall into place. No. I was anxious about Ben and me. Or not Ben and me. Was there a Ben and me? I kept having dreams about him. Not full sex or anything. But kissing. And being places with him, and looking for him, and trying to catch trains and Tubes to get to him, and events and things and people getting in the way. Sally would say I had it bad – really bad.

But I couldn't help it. Keeping my hands off him was so hard. It was as though they were magnetic, and kind of attracted to him all on their own. I was sure he liked me too – he'd said so, hadn't he, the other night? That night in another cab.

The taxi drove around until we got to the entrance. He dropped us off right outside. I was glad we were in a decent car – a Merc. I thought about being Nicole Kidman as I stepped out on to the pavement. Or maybe Gwyneth Paltrow. They'd be restrained and demure and certainly not trip over, like I was trying not to.

It was fine anyway, because Ben helped me from the car like gentlemen do in old films. Those gents wouldn't leave a girl to bundle herself haphazardly out of a limo showing everything to the world like Britney and Paris.

There wasn't a red carpet up to the doors, and there weren't any paparazzi, but I felt as though I was as good as royalty, walking up with Ben, knowing I looked fantastic – thanks to Nita. Instead of falling over I was walking on clouds.

'Mr and Mrs Beaumont-Dillon,' Ben said confidently to the doorman, who scanned his clipboard list, running a pen up and down it.

'Sorry, sir, they appear to be here already. Can I see your invitation?'

I thudded down to earth, and in that moment my impulse was to run for it. Take Ben's hand and run away. Pretend we hadn't been trying to blag our way into a bash we weren't supposed to be at. Forget all about this silly story, just like Dad had said. But I stood still, tried not to shake, and swallowed. It would be OK. It would be OK. It would be OK . . .

'Er, here it is,' said Ben. 'There must be some mistake – because we're definitely out here, and not inside!' he joked.

The doorman gave a forced smile. He must have heard all this before – chancers trying their luck at getting into a posh event. 'That all looks in order. Let me double-check with my colleague – I wasn't on the door when the other couple arrived.' He got out a walkie-talkie and turned away as he spoke into it: 'Hey there, John. A couple – the Beaumont-Dillons – was that you let them in, you dozy git?

Really? No one by that name rings a bell? Any chance you might have crossed off the wrong name? Not beyond the realm of possibility? Yeah? OK. I'll sort it.'

It would be OK . . .

He clipped the walkie-talkie back on his belt. 'Daft bastard,' he muttered under his breath.

'I must apologise, Mr Beaumont-Dillon, but my colleague appears to have made a mistake. Do come in with your lady wife and have a lovely evening.'

'Thank you,' said Ben, in his best I-could-be-an-Internet-millionaire-for-all-you-know voice. 'I'm sure you're just doing your job . . .'

We caught each other's eye. It was all we could do not to collapse in giggles when we were through into the lobby. Part relief, part the cheekiness of what we were doing.

Signs led us along corridors and up stairs, and then we were there. The babble of voices spilt out of the room. Doors opened on to marble and glass and a deck of thick, deep armchairs with low tables. But what I craved to see was outside. This was the Pitch View Room, and it lived up to its name. Through the deep windows there it was – bright green, almost luminous in the evening light – the sacred turf of Wembley. The totemic white arch reached high above us, held not quite vertical by thick steel cables.

'You like?' asked Ben, handing me a glass of champagne.

'It's great,' I replied. 'Of course it would be even better with an England game going on, but this is still . . . pretty good.'

'Come on, we need to work the room now,' said Ben. 'See if we can track down anyone on our "most wanted" list.'

I wasn't sure where to start. All these men in penguin suits looked very much the same. It was going to be tougher than I'd imagined: 'Oh, we'll just go in and spot them and listen in to their conversation, and work out who the government guy is and then do a high five and it'll all be sorted.' No, it wasn't going to be like that.

Ben and I tried to move through the room as systematically as possible, smiling and attempting to blend in and not look too suspicious. Which is a little tricky when you're staring at people and wondering if you recognise them. What if I was missing one of our targets simply because he had a bad photo on the company website?

I felt as though we'd been round the whole room at least three times. The sun was going down outside, and still no luck. I'd seen three TV stars and a sprinkling of politicians, and someone who I thought was a big-shot businessman, although I wasn't sure of his name. But no one who matched our mugshots.

Waiters and waitresses brought round silver trays filled with tiny morsels, and a tower of napkins. I kept asking what was in the canapés, and after a while my favourite waiter, a boy with blond hair who was probably about my age, made sure to tell me as soon as he arrived which things I could eat and which I wouldn't like.

'Do you think this is giving me away?' I asked Ben. 'The fact I'm snarfing down all these canapés?'

'I don't think anyone's noticed. Except the people who haven't had a mouthful yet, because you've eaten it all.'

'And I had some supper at Nita's as well . . .' I looked down at my stomach. It wasn't, like, bulging out, but maybe I'd better stop. At least I hadn't spilt anything on myself. Not yet. Do you know how hard it is to eat and drink while you're standing up with a glass in one hand and a napkin in the other, and trying not to drop the whole lot down your front? Well, I found it a challenge.

And then I spotted someone I did know. It was James Hepworth, over beyond a group of loud blokes who sounded too posh for their own good: 'Yah, yah, yah.' Ben had said Mr Pinstripe wasn't coming, but if he was here maybe that meant he wanted to help us some more.

I felt relieved. Surely he would lead us to the guilty person. Even if he couldn't – or wouldn't – reveal his government contact, he'd be bound to be talking to the Auricle directors, so then we'd know who to tail.

Except that the person he was bent over in conversation with wasn't from Auricle.

18

I dashed behind Ben and held him in front of me, like a human shield. 'Over there, talking to James – it's Dad,' I whispered – only it was quite a loud whisper, on account of I was so shocked.

'What? Your father? But—'

'I know – what's he doing here? I'm getting a bad feeling about this, Ben. Let's get out of here.'

We tried to make a dignified exit. Ben made up some story at the door about me needing some fresh air, so we got passes to be let back in again.

'We can't just stand in the corridor – what if Dad comes out?' I said.

'OK, let's go down there,' said Ben, pointing to a fire exit door that was ajar. We edged through.

'Do you have any idea why your dad's here?' Ben asked.

'No. I mean, I knew he was in London, but he said he was meeting some "colleagues". What if he's, you know . . .' I didn't want to finish the sentence. There must be some innocent explanation of why Dad was here and why he'd lied about it to me. But he had been funny on the phone. Talking about needing to keep secrets from me about something. What if he was implicated in all of this in some way?

We carried on walking down corridors and stairways. And suddenly there we were, emerging into Wembley Stadium, stack upon stack of seats rising above us, and the pitch, close-cropped and manicured, below. Sprinklers were washing it in a fine rain of water. The grass had more or less recovered from the thousands of boots pounding it over the season, but it needed coddling against the effects of drought. I wondered if Wembley got exemption from hose-pipe bans.

For a moment all thoughts of dirty gold and government conspiracies flew out of my head. Wembley. I felt a surge of elation as I lifted my head to take in the heights of the stadium. The sun was setting and the white of the buildings and the arch was turning apricot.

'It's beautiful, isn't it?' I said to Ben. But he didn't have a chance to answer, because right then a security man appeared practically next to us, almost like a conjuring trick. I jumped. 'Shit,' said Ben, under his breath.

'Sir, madam, I'm afraid this area is out of bounds. Can I escort you back to your party?'

Sheepishly we followed him back. What if there was a big fuss and everyone – including my dad – glued their eyes on to us? What if they found out we weren't supposed to be there? What if we were arrested or something? Please don't let that happen.

It didn't, but the security guard did frisk us – very politely

– in a side room before shepherding us back in. And he searched my borrowed evening bag, turning everything over carefully and opening all my borrowed make-up. I was glad I'd remembered Ben's advice to make sure I had no ID on me.

When we got back in the room my dad was nowhere to be seen. I didn't know whether to be relieved or worried. What should we do now? I mean, if Dad was the 'government official' there was no point staying here – I had to confront him. But what if he wasn't and it was a coincidence that he was here? Or what if he was involved but covering up for someone else who was still here, and who he'd maybe tipped off?

'We should carry on looking here. It's logical,' Ben declared with a serious face. 'We know where your dad's going to be – on his way back to his flat, or to Bath. We don't need to follow him. But if he's not the one we're after, we could lose our opportunity if we leave now.'

He had a point. So we were staying.

'I'm going to try and talk to James. You stay here and keep a watch,' said Ben.

The champagne was still flowing, so I snaffled another glass, and then drank it too quickly, the bubbles fizzing on my tongue. I sat down for a while, trying to be inconspicuous.

To be honest, my feet were beginning to complain about being in such high shoes. I wished I could take them off, and run barefoot over the cool grass of the Wembley pitch.

'Mind if I sit down?' said a voice at my shoulder.

Oh no. The last thing I needed – someone I'd have to make conversation with and pretend I was Mrs Beaumont-Dillon. 'No, that's fine,' I replied, with what I hoped was a sweet-but-grown-up smile.

'Timothy Green,' said a man who looked, well, just like a businessman: oldish, greying, thinning hair, paunch. He held out his hand for me to shake.

'C-Claudia Beaumont-Dillon,' I said in my turn. (Please let him go away soon.)

'Charmed. I hope I'm not disturbing you. Only I thought I'd come over here and admire the view,' he said, looking out of the window into the stadium.

'Oh, yes, it's fantastic, isn't it?' (Oh, no, he wasn't going to start a conversation, was he?) I tried to make my voice sound posher than normal. Maybe if I imagined I was one of those airhead Z-list celebrities who hang out on the fringes of royalty. That should help: 'Ditzy Claudia – she's a charming little filly, used to come to Mahiki and Boujis all the time before she got hitched to that Internet millionaire fellow – one of William or Harry's chums, I think he is. Or maybe he's one of those riff-raff made good – one of our friends in the North . . .'

My new friend settled himself into a leather chair and sighed. 'That's better,' he said. 'My colleagues over there are all talking shop, and I'd rather like a night off from business.'

I glanced over in the direction he'd indicated with his head. Among the laughter and joviality one cluster of men was looking more focused, with more furrowed brows. 'Oh, right,' I ventured. (Perhaps if I just said 'Oh' and 'Mm' now and again I could devote most of my brain to having a nice fantasy about playing football at Wembley, and the post-match shower, and perhaps Ben having to come in it with me . . .)

There was a pause where I tried to keep a friendly smile going, but also a faintly detached aura that said 'I'd-like-my-own-space-please'. It didn't work.

'I hope you don't mind, but I was just admiring your jewellery . . .' (Admiring my jewellery? That was a strange chat-up line – unless he was a jewel thief or something.)

'This?' I said, my hand coming up to the necklace Nita had acquired for me. I'd said no gold, so this was a concoction of pearls and silver. Or maybe platinum. I hoped it wasn't platinum, because then I'd have to start getting paranoid about not losing it.

'Yes. I see you're a pearls-and-platinum girl. But I do think gold would better suit your complexion.' (Maybe he was in fashion or something, but he really didn't look the type.)

'Really?' (Or maybe . . .) 'Are you in the gold business – I mean, I was wondering how you know about jewellery.'

'That's very perceptive of you. In fact, yes I am. But I'm not biased – gold really would suit you better. And especially a rose gold, I'd say.'

(But he wasn't on our 'most wanted' list, or I'd have remembered. So perhaps he was with another company.)

'A friend of mine is a jewellery designer.' (Yeah, like who?

But I needed the fib to keep the conversation informal – not like an interrogation session.) 'She might have talked to me about your company . . . What's . . .?'

'The name? I doubt she'll have dealings with us, but we're called Auricle. Ring any bells?'

I didn't even flinch. 'Yes. No. Perhaps. I'm not sure. Is it a large company then?' (Yes, yes, yes!)

'Quite large. But it's all very boring what we do. More about the business side of gold, not the glamorous jewellery side.' (Boring? Certainly not to me.)

'Please excuse me, but I need to visit the Ladies. And then I think I'd better find my husband – he seems to have wandered off.'

'Lovely to meet you. Remember what I said about rose gold, and give it a try.'

I couldn't see Ben as I dodged past couples and groups towards the loos. I went in, closed the door of a cubicle and jumped up and down with delight. It was as good as scoring a winning goal. But I had to tell Ben so he (or we) could tail Timothy's colleagues before they slunk off home to consider their guilty consciences. Not that they had any, probably. I unfolded the paper with our smudgy mugshots – which thankfully the security guard hadn't noticed in the little side pocket of my make-up bag – and tried again to imprint the faces even deeper in my head: sandy hair here, black-framed glasses there, a bulgy nose, one who looked a bit like an older Graham Norton.

When I found Ben I was like a puppy dog, eagerly

tugging at his sleeve. He'd been caught up in conversation with someone who was also talking to James Hepworth. It all sounded very tedious, although it was amusing hearing Ben try to bluff about dotcoms.

'Hello, darling,' Ben said, and pulled me close. 'This is my wife, er, Claudia,' he announced to James and his companion. 'Can you excuse us for a moment?'

I found us a quietish corner from which we could survey Timothy and his mates – the blokes with frowns. It was obvious now that I knew. There was at least one face I recognised from the creased paper.

'So now we watch them like hawks, right?' I asked Ben.

'That's right, just like large birds of prey,' he answered.

'Did you get anything from James?'

Ben shook his head. 'Nothing. I think he was just enjoying making me act out my cover story. He kept introducing me to anyone who came over. The bastard.'

As I fixed my steely gaze on the Auricle crew I caught Ben looking at me. 'If you're my wife . . .' he began. 'If you're my wife, does that mean I can kiss you?'

'I suppose so,' I said, still staring at my prey but half-distracted by thoughts I shouldn't be having. 'But not now, because I'm concentrating . . . Come on, take this seriously, Ben. We're working here.' I wasn't really serious, it was banter, teasing – taunting perhaps. There's nothing I'd have liked better than for Ben to kiss me. But not then. Later.

Ben and I pretended to be talking, and Ben got more drinks for us, and then another for himself, and another. I was trying to be sensible and have lots of water. But I wondered how much Ben was drinking. He had his arm around my waist and where it touched against me the skin felt hypersensitive.

We watched and waited, and waited and watched. Ben kept up a commentary about the people at the party: 'There's a guy over there, he could be a dead ringer for Mr Bean. He must be pissed as a fart. He's just dropped his phone on the floor and then tripped over picking it up . . . And there's a woman to my right who makes Jordan look tasteful. God, what is she wearing? Bright yellow? And I dread to think what I'll see if she bends over . . . And there's a bloke who looks like Ken Clarke – you know, the old Tory guy – he's practically asleep on his feet. Any moment now his eyelids are going to flop shut . . .'

Well, it kept us amused. And took our minds off the fact that we hadn't seen anyone suspicious talking to our targets.

'Shall we go soon?' Ben whispered into my hair. 'Maybe we've missed our government suspect.'

'Or maybe it is my dad,' I added gloomily. It looked as though we had two unappealing options – either we'd failed, or else my dad was the government nasty we were after.

'Hang on,' said Ben, suddenly alert, and pulling away from me slightly. 'James looks as though he wants me to go over . . . Don't turn round,' he added as I started to crane my head. 'I'll just go and see what he wants. Maybe he's ready to cough up the name this time.'

Ben walked over to James, and I perched on the wide

back of one of the chairs. Perhaps it wasn't going to be all bad this evening. And then I felt as though someone was looking at me. You know the feeling: my neck and back felt kind of tense and tingly. I flicked my head round and there was this man with dark hair and a weaselly face – narrow and pointed, with small brown eyes. He smiled a slow smile as he saw me looking at him. Creepy. What was he after?

I turned back to check on Tim's Auricle mates, but when I looked again Mr Weasel was gone. I knew I hadn't imagined him – had I?

19

The insistent caterwauling of an alarm shrieked through my head. *Squeal, squeal, squeal* . . . I looked around for Ben, and everyone else in the room was swivelling their heads about too. Some faces were anxious, some were calm. Then, like sheep brought to heel by a well-trained shepherd dog, everyone started to push towards the door. The security guards were telling us all not to panic – it was most probably a false alarm, but we did need to follow the procedure. All file out quietly now, please, ladies and gentlemen. Leave your jackets and bags in the cloakroom, you'll be able to collect them later . . . But of course loads of people wanted their bags and briefcases (some must have come straight from work), and started to scramble in among the hangers and chains holding their belongings.

I was caught up in the flow towards the closest exit door. I spotted Ben's head, and he waved at me as he was carried towards the opposite one. I tried to check if James or any of the Auricle people were close by, but I wasn't tall enough, even in my heels. Heads and beards and soft bellies and perfumed dresses pressed around me. I was looking forward to getting out into the air.

Squeal, squeal, squeal . . . The alarm still pulsed in my ears.

We clip-clopped down stairs and through fire doors until we emerged into a car park. People stood in little huddles, talking loudly, and wondering to each other what had made the alarm go off. Fire? Terrorists? Prank? Something gone wrong with the system?

I couldn't see any sign of Ben. But Timothy Green was there. He smiled at me, so I smiled back. He was with a couple of the Auricle people. Maybe I should go over and introduce myself – try the direct approach. Do like on those documentaries where the reporter doorsteps their subject, then has to run alongside them, dragging along the film crew (or secret camera) as their prey tries to run away as quickly as possible to the sanctuary of their car. The subject always looks bad, and desperate. But then they deserve to, usually.

It would have been great to have a hidden camera. Though not really possible in this dress. Maybe it could be discreetly wired up in my bag.

Ben was still nowhere to be seen. My feet were hurting.

And then there was another face I recognised. A face at a doorway. It was Mr Weasel. I wished Ben were around, so we could see if he recognised him. What was the Weasel up to? I'd disliked him straight away. And then he'd done that disappearing act, just before the alarm went off . . .

Most people were looking up at the building, or talking to

those around them, but I had my eyes fixed in another direction. If Mr Weasel did anything, I'd know about it. I didn't think he'd noticed me watching him, or he probably wouldn't have done what he did next – which was to show me that he had to be involved in this dirty gold business, right up to his weaselly neck.

Mr Weasel was holding open a door – one marked 'Staff Only' – and beckoning several men through. They were the Auricle directors. One, two, three of them, trying to look casual as they walked towards him. I really wished I had a hidden camera then.

But I did have the next best thing. I took out my phone and snapped some pictures. You couldn't see a lot in them, but maybe it would be possible to do something on a computer. I sent them to Ben – and Sally too. I mean, I'm not paranoid, but just in case anything should happen to us (like being arrested) or to our phones I thought someone else should have the evidence. Someone a long way from here. I hoped Sally didn't erase them or anything. I'd have to text later with an explanation.

Mr Weasel looked around before he closed the door. And then he saw me. I froze. I just stood there, stupidly, my feet not moving. His look sent a chill through me. Again, I remembered those words that James had spoken, when I only knew him as Mr Pinstripe, on a train, what seemed like a lifetime ago.

'No, no, no. They must not find out. We can't let that happen. OK? Do what you have to . . .'

I knew now that he hadn't meant them as badly as I'd thought. But with Mr Weasel? I really couldn't be sure.

As soon as Ben reached me I told him everything. We rushed to the door that the Weasel and his cronies had disappeared into, but it was locked. We tried to find another way back in, but the security guards wouldn't let us. (So why had they allowed Mr Weasel in? It seemed as though everybody was caught up in this conspiracy.)

'Let's have a look at the pictures,' said Ben, as we sat on the step of the 'Staff Only' door. We looked at them on my mobile, because Ben said it had a better screen than his (which was ancient because he hadn't got around to upgrading it).

He screwed up his eyes to peer at the photo. Then he listened to my description.

'Sorry, Becks, but I can't tell who it is from this.' I was disappointed. I'd wanted him to know straight away who our culprit was. But then he made a suggestion that definitely perked me up.

'Look, there's no point us hanging around here any more, is there? Let's jump in a cab, take this picture back to my place and see if we can get a better idea when we blow it up. OK?'

My heart did a flip. That sounded more than OK.

In the taxi I wasn't sure what to do. Should I cuddle up close, like that last time? Ben had said nothing was happening, but tonight you wouldn't have believed that. If anything, it had been him wanting to, you know, kiss me. Maybe he was coming round to the idea. I mean, seventeen isn't that young, is it? There are people with children at seventeen, and jobs, and getting married. But I didn't want to fling myself at him and then feel stupid. So I sat there, upright, trying to keep at least a few millimetres between us, while the cab driver engaged Ben in a conversation about whether the site for the Olympics was going to be finished in time. (How could Ben be interested in talking to a cab driver when he could be snogging me?)

I started out trying to be interested in what they were saying, but then I gave up and drifted into my own thoughts.

So if Mr Weasel was the government no-gooder, then that must mean my dad was off the hook. But still, why on earth had he been there? What was he doing? And he'd seemed very keen for me to stop following this story. Perhaps he was covering for someone, or not telling the whole truth, or trying to work out how to spin the story so the government wouldn't look so bad.

Or perhaps he was genuinely trying to protect me. He knew from experience that these were unpleasant people, who would do anything to protect themselves – except, perhaps, poisoning someone with a radioactive cup of tea – and he wanted to make sure I was out of the picture. That sounded more like the Dad I knew.

But what if the Dad I knew wasn't the real Dad – what if there were lots of things I didn't actually know about him? It all made me feel very queasy. I supposed I should talk to him. But something was holding me back. A part of me that didn't want to have everything out in the open, in case there was the faintest possibility of hearing something I didn't want to. And anyway, if Dad had been less than honest with me, who was to say he wouldn't lie again, even if I confronted him?

'. . . And if you pull up here – that's right, in front of that van – that would be great. Ta.'

I hadn't really been taking in our route, but now we were in a narrow street of terraced shops and houses.

'Where's this?' I asked.

'Brick Lane,' Ben replied. 'Or just off it really.'

It was late in the evening but there were still people wandering about, especially along the street at the end of the road. That must be Brick Lane, then. There was a fake, jokey shriek from a youngish woman in a short denim skirt and stripey leggings. She lurched into the bloke she was walking with and they started to kiss, her head tipped up towards his. They were probably about Ben's age, I thought to myself.

Ben was still in the cab, pulling cash out of his pockets.

I got out and stood in the road. The air was humid. It felt as though a thunderstorm could be on the way. A tight cap of pressure gripped around my skull and there was a strange smell on the breeze, like damp dust. Then, in the distance, I heard a low rumble. A big, fat drop of rain slapped on to the pavement. And then another.

There were more shrieks, coming from Brick Lane, and

people started to run for cover. I let the water drip on to me. I love the feel of a thunderstorm after a blistering hot day – the cool relief of the raindrops; the excitement of the lightning; the menacing thunder roar. They make me want to run as fast as I can through the streets, or fields, or wherever. And I would have dragged Ben out of the car and made him run with me then, except for . . .

'My dress!' I'd forgotten I was wearing a hugely expensive piece of clothing that had to be returned in perfect condition, or else Nita would get into all kinds of trouble. 'Ben, quick, I need to get inside. Or else the rain – I don't know what it'll do to it.'

Ben fumbled with his door key, and then we were in the hall of his shared flat. Panic over. Not too much rain had got on my party frock. We edged along a narrow corridor and up some narrow stairs. The flat was above a shop that sold fancy garden stuff and perfumes.

'There's my flatmate's room, and the bathroom, and the kitchen-cum-sitting room at the back there. Then my room's up those stairs, in the attic,' said Ben, pointing out the main features. 'Sorry about the mess but, you know, well, it's two boys sharing, so you get the picture.'

'No problem,' I said, looking around me at the posters of bands and exhibitions on the walls.

'D'you fancy a beer? Or I've got the end of some wine in the fridge . . .'

'Maybe some wine,' I said, already knowing it was probably a bad idea. Well, I could leave it if I started feeling all swimmy and sick. Although I'd maybe like to avoid actually being sick. I didn't think that was really the way to impress Ben.

Ben went to the fridge and I hung around in the hall. I really should change out of this dress and check it was all still OK. The problem was, I didn't have anything else to wear. I took a peek into the bathroom. There was a complete lack of anything girly. Just razors and Imperial Leather soap and some kind of shaving gel stuff.

'Here you go,' said Ben, handing me a glass filled to the brim. 'Why don't you come and sit down? I won't bite, you know.'

'It's just . . .' I started. 'The thing is, I need to change out of this dress before I wreck it – or so I can make sure I haven't wrecked it already. But I don't have anything to wear.'

'Ah. I see the problem,' said Ben. He hesitated for a moment, then: 'Why don't you come upstairs and we'll see what we can find.'

Obediently, I walked up the steps behind him. Now, I'd be lying if I said there wasn't some sexual tension in the air at this point. I kept looking at Ben, and he kept looking at me. And all I could see were his deep grey eyes, and all I could remember was how it had felt when we were so close that time before. Everything we said hung in the air, as though there was a secret code going on between us. Except that – could I be sure that's what was happening? What if I was misreading it all? Sally always says I'm rubbish at knowing when people fancy me, and terrible at giving out mixed signals so boys don't know where they stand. Maybe I was doing that here. If only Ben would make a move, then I'd know for sure.

He found me a T-shirt, and a pair of trackie bottoms that he said had shrunk in the wash, and maybe that would mean they'd fit me OK.

I went to take them downstairs, to change in the loo. 'It's OK, you can change up here. I'll go . . .' said Ben. But then he didn't go. 'Do you need a hand with the zip?'

It was such a lame line I couldn't believe Ben was saying it. But I felt zingy with anticipation.

'Maybe,' I said. 'OK.' And I turned so that my back was towards him. Ben pulled the zip slowly down to the bottom. And then he stroked my back, and slid his hand between the silky fabric and my skin.

Yes, yes, yes. I so wanted this. I sooo wanted it. My whole body wanted it. I so wanted Ben.

I twisted around to face him and Ben kissed me then. Gently at first over my cheeks and eyelids. And then he grabbed my hair in his fist and kissed me properly and hard.

When we came up for air, panting, he looked intensely into my eyes. 'I really shouldn't be doing this,' he said.

And then, 'I really shouldn't be doing this,' he repeated as he buried his face in my neck, and pushed me back on to his bed.

The rain drummed on the roof and misted through the open window. Every so often the room was lit with bright blue-white and resounded with gun-cracks of thunder.

20

It's not like I'd never had sex before or anything.

Sally says that Zak broke my heart and I need to get over it. Maybe it's time to tell you all about that.

It started in Cornwall. We were on a football tour during the Easter holidays. That was over a year ago, but it's one of those things, it could have been yesterday or it could have happened to another person. It feels kind of unreal. Except that it still hurts to think about it.

I met Zak on one of our days off, in a place called Widemouth Bay (pronounced Widmuth, Zak corrected me later) near Bude; a long, wide beach with rocky cliffs at each end. Sally and I were eating ice-creams as the wind whipped our faces, and watching the surfers.

They looked like little stick figures, paddling out through the waves or upright on their boards, silhouetted against the sky. Some only managed a few seconds before they tumbled into the water, but others seemed glued on, looping and dipping with the waves.

Late in the afternoon, with the sun shining low over the water, two surfers walked up the beach in our direction, boards under their arms. I squinted in the sunlight, and I could swear the shorter one smiled at me. He had blue eyes with a touch of aqua, and sun-gold hair slicked back from his face by the sea. But then he was away up the beach and gone.

I thought that was the last I'd see of him, but just as the minibus was about to take us back to the campsite two heads appeared at the door.

'Any chance of a lift into town?' asked my surfer, with a grin.

Zak visited our campsite secretly that evening, and I fell completely in love. I thought he did too. Neither of us said, but I *knew* that he loved me.

He came to see me back in Bath, and I persuaded Mum and Dad to let me go to Cornwall. We spent all the time we could together.

Then, over the summer holidays, came the evening of the beach party. It was the kind of evening you never forget; it's seared in your psyche forever. There was firelight and smoky barbecue food and cold beers. It was so dreamy. So special. Zak and I wandered off along the beach. We knew what we wanted to do.

The next day I felt so different. I felt like a woman, not a girl. All day I couldn't forget what we'd done the night before. My whole body was shouting: 'I've had sex! With a really cute boy! And I love him!'

Zak and I carried on seeing each other but later, when I talked about coming to Bude in the break after Term One, he said how maybe it wasn't such a good idea. He kept trying to put me off. At first it was annoying and we rowed; but then he stopped calling or messaging and it was agony. I moaned and moped about so much that Sally was tearing her hair out.

In the end I found out from his friends that Zak had been seeing someone else. Perhaps even while we were still sleeping together.

So that's my sob story.

Ben's pillow smelled of Ben and Ben's leg was resting against mine. Reluctantly I drew myself away and looked around for something to wear so I could go to the toilet. I found the T-shirt and trackie bottoms, and retrieved my party dress from the floor. It didn't look too bad, but the blind was drawn shut so I couldn't really see properly. Then I tiptoed out. Ben was still fast asleep, with his mouth open.

Last night he'd kept asking me if I was sure I wanted to. And I kept having to say yes I was – even though I was a little bit nervous. And I didn't know whether I should ask if he had condoms (he did).

I had to put down the toilet seat before I could have a pee (boys sharing a flat again). I felt alert and awake; maybe ready to start all over again.

I climbed back into bed. It was cold on the side where I'd got out, but all warm next to Ben. I snuggled up close to him and looked over the horizon of his chest. It rose and fell as he breathed, blocking out part of my view of his room and then revealing it again.

He started to stir.

'Hi there,' he said, eyes half closed.

'Hi,' I replied.

'What time is it?' Ben rolled over and reached for the alarm clock on the floor by his bed. 'Ten. Five past ten,' he read out, answering his own question.

I'd taken off the trackie bottoms, but I was still wearing Ben's T-shirt. 'You look good in that,' he added. 'Sexy.'

'Really?' I had a wide, happy grin.

Ben kissed me on the forehead. 'I'm starving. Do you like bagels?' But as he was saying this he was running his hand down the T-shirt and over my breast.

'Mm, that sounds good.'

'OK, then.' And suddenly he was up and out of bed and pulling on a pair of jeans so quickly I hardly got a look at him.

'Have a shower if you like, I won't be long,' he called as he ran down the stairs.

I lay back down and wrapped myself in the duvet. There wasn't much in his room. Some built-in wardrobes with clothes trying to escape from them. A wood and metal desk with his computer on it. An old chair stacked with pieces of paper and newspapers and magazines. A set of shelves filled with CDs and books. Nothing on the walls up here. Nothing marking it out as particularly Ben's room – except for a Bradford City scarf draped across the window.

And then my phone rang. Or perhaps it was Ben's. No, it was mine: buzzing away inside my bag on the floor.

I got up to see if it was Ben calling because he couldn't bear to be away from me for five seconds. But it was my parents. I wavered – did I really feel like speaking to them? But I wanted to know if my dad had definitely gone back to Bath.

It was my mum. She was asking if I was coming home this weekend. Her voice sounded sharp, as though she had already decided to be angry with me. I told her I wanted to stay in London for the weekend. She went quiet.

'Fine,' she said. 'If that's what you want . . .'

I could hear the pent-up tension in her voice. What was going on? Had she and Dad had another row? I told her it was what I wanted, and then hung up before it had a chance to turn into a proper argument.

When Ben came back I was sitting straight up in his bed, irritated with myself that I'd even answered the call. 'What's wrong with you?' he asked.

I explained, and Ben told me to forget about my parents and come and have the best bagels in the whole world.

They were still warm: smooth crust on the outside, soft and white inside. Ben made coffee and poured orange juice. But we were quiet and awkward over breakfast. The spell of the night before was broken.

'So, what shall we do today?' I asked, imagining spending the whole weekend with Ben in a dreamy kind of loved-up state.

'I don't know,' he said. And then, 'Shouldn't you go back to your dad's flat, change into some of your own clothes?'

It wasn't the answer I'd been looking for. 'I suppose so,' I said, thinking, *but if we're in bed I won't need clothes*. But I didn't say it.

'How about I call you a cab after breakfast?'

'I'll be fine on the Tube,' I said. 'Really. But we can have some more time together before I go back, can't we?'

'Yeah,' said Ben. 'Of course. But I've, er, I've, you know, got some things I need to do today.'

'Oh. All right.' This wasn't going well.

It was much better when Ben suggested he show me round Brick Lane. He took me to the bagel bakery, to get me another (smoked salmon and cream cheese) for lunch, because I'd gobbled up the breakfast bagels so quickly. We laughed and talked about nonsense that we both for some reason found hilarious. We looked in fashion shops and a place with leather belts and bags, and an old warehousey building that had a kind of arts space with cafés and stuff. And then up the other end we passed by sari shops and the curry restaurants that Brick Lane is famous for – so many of them, all trying hard to look different, but all with the same menu (or that's how it seemed to me).

My arm was linked through Ben's and I took every opportunity to lean myself against him. It was like we were going out. Like he was my boyfriend.

And then I made the mistake of asking about what Nita had told me. Perhaps it was over-confidence, or perhaps I was testing him, without really knowing it myself.

'There's something Nita said she overheard,' I started.

'Yeah?'

'It was something about you and me. Do you want me to tell you?'

'Of course. What was it?'

'Well, she said that she'd heard you only wanted to get to know me because of my dad. Because he's an MP and you thought you could get some good stories off me. I mean, I know it's not true but . . .'

Ben had stopped walking.

'What? It's not true is it, so . . .'

'Becky . . . Oh Becky.' Ben was looking uncomfortable. 'There are so many things I love about you, and now that I know you I'd never ask you to . . . But . . . Shit – why am I telling you this? I could lie and say it wasn't true, or laugh it off and not even answer the question, and you'd never know. How stupid am I?'

'You mean . . .'

'It's not like you think. Really. But when I first met you I did think, my luck's in here. She's bright and pretty – and her dad's an MP.'

'So it wasn't anything to do with me having that story in the paper, and it being so brilliant like you said when we talked that evening, at Jennifer's birthday party? It wasn't because you thought I had such great potential to be a really good journalist?'

'No, that's not what I meant,' Ben said, gnawing at his thumb uncomfortably. 'I did think that . . . I do. And if you hadn't had that piece in the paper, I'd almost certainly have never known who you were at all, and never come over and talked to you.'

I couldn't believe what I was hearing. Tears were making my eyes feel full and hot. I was about to stomp off down the street. But then Ben came and wrapped me up in his arms and kissed me. 'Becky, don't be angry . . . You can trust me, you know.'

'I don't know. It's like you're not exactly who I thought you were. I thought you were straight with me.' But I didn't push him away. We kissed some more, and I felt better. For the moment.

'I'm so sorry,' he said. 'I never meant to hurt you. But I'm a journalist, it's one of those ways your mind works. Are you OK?'

Stupidly I nodded. Perhaps if I'd sobbed and shouted he'd have felt we had to go back to his flat. But as it was he kept on walking me to the Tube.

There it was, just up ahead: Whitechapel station. He came with me down to the platform. Perhaps he didn't want to let go either. And then my train came in and he didn't ask me to stay, so I got on. I waved and blew him a kiss through the window. As the train drew away the cord between us pulled and broke, leaving my heart aching.

21

Ben texted to say he would call me later. I waited and waited. Then I texted to ask what he was doing, with lots of kisses Stuff, he replied. Bxxx. That wasn't nearly enough xxxs.

I moped about Dad's flat. I started trying to write my blog. And then I realised: we'd gone all the way to Ben's house, and not done what we were supposed to. We hadn't looked at the picture from my phone.

I squinted at the tiny screen. I had to admit that if I hadn't seen Mr Weasel in the flesh I wouldn't be able to recognise that it was him. I needed to enlarge the image.

But I didn't have a cable to connect my phone to the computer, and anyway I wasn't techy enough to work out what to do. I Googled to see if there was anything helpful online, but there were so many results to trawl through that I gave up. I had a look in Dad's Favourites – sometimes he bookmarked useful stuff like that – but there was nothing. Except I found a folder with some online poker sites. I didn't know Dad was into that kind of thing.

I so didn't want to wash the smell of Ben off me, but in

the end I gave in and had a shower. I put my phone on the floor beside the bath so I wouldn't miss any calls from Ben. Then I was hungry so I raided the last morsels that were left in the flat: a tin of baked beans and some sliced bread in the freezer. I kept the phone on the counter. I sat down to eat and switched on the TV, and laid my phone on the sofa next to me.

When a message flashed up I nearly jumped through the roof. But it wasn't Ben. It was Jake, asking if I wanted to go and see Sharpedge play that night. I texted back to say I couldn't, thinking I would almost certainly be out on a date then.

My blog entry for Sunday 3 August:

. . . so nothing more's happened with uncovering the dirty gold scandal since i wrote yesterday. i have to identify mr weasel.

what some of u will be more interested in – those of you who don't enjoy the politics – is what's happening (or not) with ben.

i wud like to start with a grovelling apology to anyone who said i shud stay as far away from ben as possible as it wud all end in tears. i don't know if it has

ended but there have certainly been tears
n i think they are all mine (so far!!).
it's all thanks to jake that i'm not a
complete sad case n spending all night n
day in the flat with weepy dvds n a box
of tissues.

ben said he wud call me but of course he
then did the boy thing n went all silent
n i got some measly txts but that was all.
there was nothing all day until it was
already the evening. i had thought - n u
can call me stupid now - that we wud
definitely be going out last night. n that
after fri evening he wud probably be my
boyfriend and then i'd be meeting his
parents n blahblahblah. i am so naïve i
shock myself sometimes. (i know uve tried
to educate me sally in the ways of the
world but somehow i always believe things
will turn out better.) of course boys r
rubbish at treating u properly - if anyone
knows that it's me - but i thought that
because ben is older he wud be different
from that other person who i'm not going
to name here.

it was really late in the afternoon n then

when ben did at last finally call he moaned on that he had some work to do n after it was a friend's birthday who i didn't know so he thought it wud be better if he went on his own. so first i thought - what work? unless it's our story n then surely i need to be there. n then i thought - why can't i meet his friends what's wrong with that? what's wrong with me? but i didn't say that i just more or less pleaded and then he said maybe we cud meet up 2morrow (which is today now) tho he cudnt promise anything because he had stuff to do sunday as well!!! i mumbled pathetically n put the phone down n prepared for an evening of misery n then jake called n we talked for ages with me sobbing but not so bad by the end.

Finally he persuaded me to go out n see sharpedge. he said nita wud be there (i didn't catch on at the time but more about that later).

at first i was mrs puffy-eyes n a bit gloomy but after a while i got into the music n sharpedge were excellent. we were supposed to have id to get in but somehow jake managed to get round that (he's nineteen anyway) because we were on the guest list or something.

it was great to see nita too. i confessed everything to her then - i hadn't called her straight away about ben because she had warned me n she had been right n i felt silly n upset. but she was v sweet n didn't say i told you so or anything she gave me a hug instead n then i noticed she was holding jake's hand!!

i don't know how i cud have missed that one but then nita hadn't said anything to me about it (how cud she be so secretive?) n not even jake fessed up before last night. i wasn't pissed off at them or anything because i think they make a perfect couple n anyway everything is sorted between nita n me now. but it did make me feel sad that ben wasn't there. it wud have been so cool.

afterwards we hung around with rich n manny tho they had to keep rushing off to talk to people about the gig n help get their kit loaded. i was soaked through -

ew! — cos it was so hot in the gig and when i went outside into the dark i felt suddenly chilly n shivery. rich lent me his jacket. he is not so tall as jake n has a nice smile when he is not posing n looking ultracool on stage. i think manny was a bit put out that nita was with jake.

i better go now because they have all arranged to meet up in camden today. i wasn't going to go but surprise surprise mr ben hutchison has not called me even tho i have left a msg this morning. i am really not going to cry my heart out over this. really.

I have been feeling so confused.

I got the Tube up to Camden and waited where Jake had said, on the corner next to the station, by the metal railings. It seemed to be a favourite meeting spot. The pavement was covered with pounded-in blobs of gum and cigarette butts. A young bloke in a grimy parka and boots with holes was sitting next to one of the cashpoint machines in the station wall. Most people tried not to look at him as they drew out their money; they hunched over the keypad as they typed in their PIN number, attempting to hide what they were keying in.

It was noisy, with traffic and blaring music from cars with

their tops down, and touts shouting out the tickets they had for sale, and a woman asking if anyone wanted to buy *The Big Issue*. A Japanese-looking boy with fluffy, spiky hair walked up and down with a neon-pink sign advertising a sportswear sale.

I felt more at home here than among the grand buildings and suits and air-conditioning of Canary Wharf.

I'd thought I was going to be late but everyone else was even later. Rich was the first to turn up and he asked how I was. I said OK. I didn't know if Jake had told him about Ben but I didn't want to go into all that so I said I thought the gig was brilliant. (Which I did. I'd decided I really liked Sharpedge's music; maybe I'd even start getting into their kind of indie/boho/mod look.)

'Really? Thanks,' said Rich. 'There were some journalists there, and record company A&R people, although we may just carry on with promoting ourselves. We've got a song out, you know? It's on my Lifetribe page – you can download it from there. If you like.'

'Yeah, I will,' I said, feeling a bit shy (Rich was practically a rock star, after all). 'I've got a page there too, with my blog . . .'

'Really?' Rich said again. 'That's cool. We could hook up as friends . . .' *Oh, no*, I thought. *Maybe I should erase all those blog spots about Ben.* And if I was going to have a wider circle of friends, perhaps I should start being more careful what I wrote there.

Then I heard 'Hi, guys' over my shoulder. It was Jake.

And soon Nita had arrived too, in another fabulous outfit of course. (Mind you, I was wearing my second purchase from our shopping frenzy up the road in Primrose Hill; it was white and quite severe in a ruffled and vintage kind of way that Nita said boys would find very sexy.)

'Manny said he couldn't make it,' Rich explained.

'OK, that's everyone then. Let's go,' said Jake. He put his arm around Nita.

The Camden streets were packed. A sea of people on the pavements; a sea of people in the road. It was mainly the 'younger generation' like us, but some olds too. There were miscellaneous groups of tourists dressed appallingly in baggy T-shirts and jeans that didn't fit properly, and then all kinds of fashions and tribes. Lots of black, of course, and mohawks and fluorescents and piercings and flesh tunnels and big boots and skin-tight trousers and tiny skirts and long skirts and chopped fringes and eyeliner. We had to push our way through to get anywhere we wanted. I could smell skunk as we passed some boys sitting on the bridge over the canal at Camden Lock.

We turned down a cobbled side way and found ourselves surrounded by market stalls. Clothes hung from beneath striped awnings and the scents of onions and incense weaved through the air. We passed a fruit juice stall and an occult jewellery stall and one with carved wooden figures and furniture from Thailand or somewhere like that. I almost walked into a strange kind of monkey-demon carving in bright reds and greens, with monstrous bulgy eyes, just at my head height. 'Aargh!' I screeched, and jumped away, on to Rich's foot.

'Ouch! Fuck. You all right?' Rich exclaimed. 'Whoah, that is scary, man,' he added when he saw the horror-monkey. We both laughed.

Nita and I went to check out some clothes while the boys spent ages searching through a record stall.

'Are you OK?' Nita asked me.

I nodded. 'I suppose. But it's just, you know, so annoying. Why can't he even call to have a proper conversation? Or come and meet me if he doesn't want me to show my face in front of his friends? I mean, I am seventeen, I'm not some little idiot kid.'

'That is so fucked up that he can't even do that,' agreed Nita. 'I know you're not going to like this, but maybe you really should just forget about him.'

'I dunno. I can't forget about Friday. It's not every day I . . . It's not every day I have an evening like that or feel like that with someone.'

I had been going to say it's not every day I have sex with someone, but I hadn't actually told Nita about the full sex bit, and I didn't want to discuss it right now, in the middle of Camden Market, while we were flicking through hangers of brightly coloured tops and vintage floral dresses.

'Oh! This would look great on you.' Nita held up a shift dress in a lovely blue. 'Try it on over your jeans.'

I looked at my reflection in the piece of mirror propped up on a chair in the corner. A mouse like girl with porcelain-pale skin and purple-and-blonde hair smiled shyly from the chair in the opposite corner, where she was sitting with her legs drawn up and feet on the seat. It must be her stall, but she didn't seem to be doing much to sell the clothes. More like watching as people came and went.

'I'm not sure,' I said. 'I do like it, but I don't know that I'm into buying anything today. Maybe I'll come back later.'

I put the dress back on its hanger, with a slight pang of regret. I knew I wouldn't be back for it.

Nita came away with two skirts and a little jacket, all at a discount. It turned out that the mousey girl was a fashion student, looking after the stall for her mother; all the best things on it, Nita said, were her designs.

As we moved on round the stalls Nita said, 'You know Rich likes you, don't you?'

I blushed. 'I had sort of picked up on that.'

'What do you think?'

'Yeah, like, he's certainly cute. But I don't know and there's still Ben . . .'

Then the boys reappeared, saying they were hungry. So we sat at a collection of benches in the middle of the market, surrounded by food stalls. There was loads of veggie stuff; I went for some Thai noodles – or that's what the sign said they were.

Rich was sitting across from me and he kept catching my eye. He was very cute. We were all talking about the bands and music we liked, and how it's such a pain when you're under eighteen and not allowed into so many things without proof you're over age. Although Rich and Jake said they both used to have fake ID.

'We're playing a festival in a couple of weeks. I could get you in if you'd like to come,' said Rich.

'Maybe—' I started. He must mean the Sun Sea Sand festival. The one I'd wanted to go to with Sally.

'That would be brilliant,' said Nita. 'Come on, Becky, let's go along. It'll be a laugh.'

Ever feel like you're being set up?

After that I began to be more self-conscious, and I kept drifting into thinking about Ben while Rich was talking to me. I ached where Ben had touched me; I wanted to be back in his bed.

The others were going on to Jake's flat, but I said I needed to get home. (I did still have my 'green cosmetics' article to finish, after all, which was a good excuse. Doesn't that seem like such a long time ago now, and in a completely different world?)

So at Chalk Farm Tube we said our goodbyes. I hugged Jake and gave him a kiss on the cheek, and did the same with Nita. Then Rich and I stood facing each other, not sure what to do next. Rich reached out and put his hands on my shoulders and I thought for a moment he was going to kiss me on the mouth, but then he touched his lips gently to my cheek. To my surprise, my heart jumped and a rush of longing swept through me.

'Bye, Becky. See you soon. I hope.'

And then he was back with the others, joking with Jake in a boysy kind of way.

I ran down the stairs to the platform, with the feeling of his kiss on my cheek, and his face instead of Ben's playing in my mind.

Like I said, I have been feeling so confused.

22

My eyes kept unfocusing from Dad's computer screen. I'd, like, been writing the same sentence for about half an hour: 'Naturegirl is pioneering a new range of green products designed especially with young women in mind, to help with problems like acne and blackheads . . .' Did that sound OK? Was what I'd typed up so far all right, or was it crap? I really couldn't tell. At this rate it would take me until I was about thirty-four to finish this piece.

I'd ask Alison to take a look at it – that would be the best idea.

And then my phone rang.

And the name flashed up.

Ben.

My head swam and my mouth went dry as I answered. Perhaps Ben was going to be massively apologetic and invite me round, but somehow I didn't have a good feeling about this call. I picked up the phone.

'Hi, Ben,' I said, trying to sound casual.

'Hi, Becky,' he replied. 'How've you been?'

'OK,' I said.

'What've you been doing?'

'Stuff.' (I hoped he got the reference to his annoying text yesterday.)

'Right,' he said. There was a pause. 'I'm sorry about not inviting you to the party, but you wouldn't have enjoyed it anyway. It was pretty much all boys. Everyone was being loud and drunk. And some of them were even talking about rugby.' Ben stopped again, I imagine so I could get his little joke about me and rugby. I didn't say anything.

'So did you go out last night?' he asked.

'Yes. I went to a gig,' I said.

'Oh. Who was playing?'

'Sharpedge.'

'I haven't heard of them, were they any good?'

This stilted small talk was excruciating. I had to make it stop.

'Ben . . .' I said. 'Look, it's quite simple. Are we going out or what? I don't mind now about why it was you first wanted to get to know me, I just need to know what's happening now. Are you trying to dump me?' I could hardly believe I'd said it. I could almost hear Sally clapping and whooping in the background.

'Becky . . . Um . . . Becky, right, see, I really do like you. Very much. And I think you're fantastic. But Friday was a mistake . . . No, I mean, not a mistake, it was amazing, but it would be a mistake to do it again. It's like, there's nine years between us. And you're still at school, and you're not even in London. It wouldn't work . . . It's not that

I don't fancy you, because I do . . .'

'. . . But not enough?' I finished.

'No. It's not that. But I really can't go out with you. I can't see it – I can't see how it could possibly work. So I think we should be friends. It's not possible otherwise. I can't do it.'

I was quiet on the end of the phone, tears rolling down my face.

'Becky?'

'We haven't even tried,' I said, in a voice that was fearfully close to being a whine of pain. 'You haven't even seen if it could work. That's not fair of you. We could at least try it for a while.'

'I'm so sorry, Becky,' said Ben. 'I didn't mean to hurt you but I can't do this.'

'So why didn't you think about that before you fucked me?' I screeched. Then I wanted to take it back. 'Sorry, sorry, I didn't mean that . . . I really like you so much, Ben. You're different, you're not like all the immature boys I meet back in Bath. We work well together, don't we? We're a great team . . . Can't we just try?'

I was ruining it now – and I had started so well, too. I felt like a girl overboard, scrabbling my hands against the side of a boat that was sailing away. Maybe it was like that film, *Titanic*, with Kate Winslet and Leo DiCaprio. Where they're parted forever.

'Becky, you're seventeen. You'll meet someone else. I'm way too old for you. The music we like is from completely different eras. We watched different TV as kids. Our friends have even less in common than we do . . .'

Ben had obviously been going over all this in his head. But it didn't work, him being sensible. I knew this stuff already, but I still wanted him.

I sniffed. There was watery snot streaming out of my nose. I wiped it on my arm.

'And I'm no good to be with. I'm bad news,' Ben continued. 'You'll hear that if you ask around. I muck up other people's lives. I'm a bastard. I don't know a good thing when I see it, and if I do then I throw it away . . .' Now he was getting dark and dramatic.

'Why don't you come over?' I said. My voice softened; I so wanted him to be here, perhaps I could talk him round. 'Come over and say goodbye here. Not on the phone.'

'No, Becky, I can't. I can't come over. Sorry. Look, I should go now. I'll see you around, OK?'

'No, why can't you . . .'

'I've got to go. Bye, Becky.'

So, was that it?

The following morning I woke to the sound of rain. Dad's flat is on the top floors of the building (like Ben's), and my room is in the attic conversion (like Ben's). I tried not to think of Ben listening to the sound of rain, just like I was.

It pounded on the roof as though it was pounding the life out of me. I didn't want to get up. And most especially I didn't want to go into the office. I didn't know what to do about anything. I wanted to slide back into unconsciousness and never come up.

I'd nearly gone round to Nita's on Sunday night; she'd suggested I should, after I spent about an hour on the phone talking about guess who. But I didn't have the energy to move by then. I was all cried out so I watched some crap TV – some show about Patricia Arquette, with a perfect blonde bob, being a medium who helps the police find serial killers. And then I had an early night.

But once I was in bed it took ages to get to sleep. And then I had these strange dreams. It was like I was the psychic, trying to find some kind of dark force that was always lurking around the corner. Ben was my boss except that sometimes he turned into Rich. And sometimes he turned into Mr Weasel, which was even more disturbing. In one scene (it was like watching a film from the inside) I was kissing Ben and then found myself in a clinch with Weasel Man. I screamed in the dream and I think I shouted out loud for real. I sat up and then had to go to the loo, and then I lay on the sheets with the rain starting to pour down. I thought I'd never get back to sleep but I must have because when I woke up it was seven o'clock.

Maybe I should throw a sickie.

But then I'd be moping around all day, not knowing what to do with myself. And I had to deliver my article to *Sunday Style*. It didn't exactly excite me, but I knew I'd regret it if I fucked that up. There was my Friday outfit to take back to Nita as well. It had just one small white wine mark on the dress – which was incredible, considering. I wrapped up the outfit as neatly as I could and put it in several layers of bags so it wouldn't get drenched.

I tried not to think about Friday. I tried very hard, but I couldn't erase it all. I dabbed my eyes with a flannel and cold water. I couldn't cry this morning; I'd look even worse than I did already.

It took me sooo looong to drag myself around and get ready. Amazingly I'd managed to do some washing on Sunday (Ben's clothes were in there), but then I'd forgotten about it and now it was twisted and rank in the machine. So that left hardly anything to wear.

Eventually I reached the Tube. Flocks of umbrellas closed their wings with relief as we all made it to the entrance. I wasn't too wet. Only the bottoms of my jeans.

The train was littered with flimsy free newspapers. Someone had left a copy of *The Times* as well. I picked it up and flicked through. I was lucky to have a seat; one advantage of living towards the southern end of the Northern line.

I don't know why I turned to the Business pages, but I did. A headline jumped out at me: 'Police to investigate gold PR scandal claims'. There was a picture of James Hepworth. So he'd gone to the police! But then I read the story, and it was very different.

The police were investigating James, not Auricle. The article said he had been arrested in possession of cocaine and there were allegations of suspected drug-dealing. He had resigned from his public relations role at Auricle as a result, the piece continued, and could face a prison sentence if convicted.

But he was about to go to Australia – why take a risk like that? From what I'd seen and learned since being here, cocaine wasn't unusual in the world of PR and journalism and political lobbying. But people didn't tend to get arrested for it. You just had to make sure your boss didn't find out (unless, of course, your boss was the one you were going to the toilets with . . .).

There was a quote from one of the Auricle directors – probably one of the men who'd been at the party on Friday – and from some guy linked to the Department of Trade and Industry, about how such a lack of professionalism was shocking and to be condemned, and gave out the wrong signals about British business and the benefits that foreign investors would find if they put their money and faith in the UK.

I felt a weight in my stomach. James had been fitted up; this had been a lesson. He hadn't been caught with drugs by any accident. Maybe he took coke and maybe he didn't, but there was no way he was a dealer, I was sure. I read the name of the government official: he was an adviser, not an MP or civil servant – which meant he was someone who wasn't elected or worked their way up the civil service; he'd been brought in specially by some government minister. I checked the name: Mr Frank Reade.

Could he be Mr Weasel?

Could this be a warning about what would happen if I went ahead with the dirty gold story?

I shuddered to think about the night Ben and I had spent being splashed all over the papers – even if I was over age, they'd find some way to make it sound immoral and sordid. Surely they couldn't know about it, but what if my dad's flat was bugged, or they'd been listening in to my phone, or Ben's? Or what if they'd somehow photographed us together? And what if my dad really was involved in some way?

Every other passenger in my carriage suddenly became a potential stalker, following every move I made to find out what I knew and anything they could use against me.

I folded the paper and stashed it in my bag. I looked from face to face along the rows of seats, and up at the people standing. To be honest it didn't seem likely. None of the faces screamed 'gold industry spy'. But then who could say what a gold industry spy would look like? My only experience was *Spooks* and Daniel Craig as 007. In the real world it wouldn't be anyone nearly so glamorous as that.

23

'It's good, Becky, you don't have to worry. I've just put some suggestions about things you could change around.' Alison gave me a big smile. 'You've definitely got a talent for this, you know.' I'd emailed her my green cosmetics article to read; it was a relief to know it was OK and I wouldn't have to panic about it not being good enough for Claire and Jan to put in the magazine.

'Thanks,' I said. 'I needed to hear that. I've been so all over the place the past few days that I couldn't tell if I was rubbish – if what I'd written was rubbish.'

'Well it's not,' Alison replied. 'And don't let anyone tell you it is – or that you are, OK?'

She was being so nice to me, I couldn't help it. I started to cry all over again.

'Becky, hey, it's all right, what's the matter?'

Alison put her arm round my shoulders and that was it. I started sobbing into her white cotton top. It smelled fresh, of the faintest fragrance of flowers. I must be all manky by comparison.

'Let's go and get a coffee, find a quiet corner in the

canteen,' she suggested.

Everything spilled out of me then. Ben, Rich, Mr Weasel, James Hepworth, my suspicions about my dad. All in no particular order. I'd needed to let it all out. Everything spinning in my head had been making me feel ill and confused.

Alison listened quietly, and she didn't seem shocked by any of it, though it must have sounded bizarre. Her eyes flicked up and her mouth twitched when I said about sleeping with Ben, but apart from that she only asked a few things when I really wasn't making sense. It was like talking to a big sister I never had – even though she was probably closer to my mum's age than mine.

When I stopped she put her arm round my shoulders and said, with understatement, 'Well, that's quite a lot you've had going on there! No wonder you're feeling confused and upset.'

'I'm sorry, I shouldn't be laying all this on you,' I said, blowing my nose on a beige canteen paper napkin.

'No problem, don't worry about it,' Alison replied.

'What should I do about Ben?' I asked.

'I think you should avoid him like the plague. But I'm maybe not the right person to speak to about Ben Hutchison – I'm not exactly an impartial witness in all this.'

'Not impartial?'

'He didn't tell you . . . ? That's so typical. Ben and I had a thing, a few months ago . . . Strange, isn't it, he can't seem to go out with women his own age, can he?'

'I didn't know. Alison, I'm sorry – you didn't say, and he didn't tell me, or I'd have . . .'

'You'd probably have done exactly the same. But I don't blame you for that. It was all over, it's just I was having problems accepting that.'

'What happened?'

'Oh the usual. His "big relationship" had ended – badly – and we got talking after work a few times, got to know each other better. Blah blah blah, we slept together, we didn't talk about it, we slept together again, still didn't talk about it, I realised I wanted more, he didn't . . . Like I say, the usual thing. I think he just wanted an affair before the next big relationship, when I wanted to be the big relationship. Cruel, hard to take, but that's reality for you.'

'Are you all right about it now?'

'Kind of, but that's not your problem. And even if Ben and I didn't have a history I'd still say to avoid him like the plague, on what you've just told me. You don't need him. You're intelligent, you're pretty, you've got much better dress sense than him.' We laughed. 'You'll meet someone much better, trust me . . .'

Hearing about how Ben had treated Alison made me angry with him, which was better than feeling mopey and sad. I really really should completely forget him.

'Now, what are we going to do about your dirty gold problem?'

My blog entry for Monday 4 August:

claire broke it to me that jan wants to hold
my article till next week cos they've got
something else that needs to go in the
magazine. i was upset but not too much. it
means i can make the changes Alison
suggested without being in a panic about it.
and anyway it being my last week here this
is maybe my last chance to get to the bottom
of what mr weasel n co have been up to.

i have decided to go ahead n continue
writing here what i know - I'll just have
to trust that none of you 'friends' are
spies for the other side! i'm not going to
be intimidated n now alison has all the
facts as well as ben so they will back me
up n make one hell of a fuss as alison put
it if anything bad about me gets anywhere
near the papers. alison said they are more
likely to offer me a load of money to shut
up or try n blackmail me in a not too
terrible way than anything really serious.

she says i shud spk to my dad right away n
tell him everything else i know n confront

him about why he was there friday. then he will be able to back me up as well. she says they might be trying to put pressure on him as a way of getting me to shut up which sounds possible and wud certainly be much better (from my point of view) than the alternative which is that he is involved in all of this n knew about it.

i looked mr frank reade up on the govt website n found out his email n office etc. so now do i contact him n say i know what u r doing? i tried to ask ben but he has not been answering my calls or msgs.

That night I stayed at Nita's. I didn't want to be on my own. Her mum made us more delicious food and Nita introduced me to Bollywood films. We tried to do the dancing and ended up collapsing in giggles.

'Rich was asking about you,' said Nita from the floor, where we were sprawling.

'He keeps texting,' I said.

'So what do you think?'

'I don't know,' I replied. 'I still don't know what I feel about Ben, and it's doing my head in thinking about Rich at the same time.'

'Why don't you follow Alison's advice and cut Ben out of your life?'

'I know I should, but I can't. Not yet. Not until he's told me face to face and I can see in his eyes that there's nothing there, that he doesn't feel anything for me.'

My blog entry for Tuesday 5 August:

went down to ben's desk yesterday to try n track him down as he's not answering phone txts email etc. but sarah said he's out of the office working on a story. he had to do an interview she said. she didn't know where - or she didn't say.

so i asked where the business editor sits n sarah showed me. i asked him what he knew about frank reade n he told me he used to work for a mining company (!). so it's starting to make sense. i kind of told him some of my suspicions n he said that it was preposterous - his word - that someone associated with the govt wud go to those lengths. but then i said surely politicians n people in power lie about stuff n try to cover it up n he agreed. he is trying to find out more from people he knows in govt n says if ben doesn't want to write the story with me then he will and will tell the editor he has to run it!!!!

It was my last four days. Nita and I had travelled in together from Stamford Hill. I didn't recognise anyone on the Tube who might be following me, but then they could have sent someone different . . .

Apart from reworking my article and looking at the photos for it there hadn't been much to do in the *Sunday Style* office so far this week. Lots of people were off on holiday, including Tallulah – which meant it was a lot quieter and calmer. It was lucky for us too, because Nita had to get the party dress cleaned and return all the stuff we'd borrowed to where it should go. Marty raised an arch eyebrow when she took the payment slips to him to be signed off, and asked if Friday night had gone well. 'No damage, I hope?' Nita assured him everything was fine.

'How are things going now?' Alison asked as I passed her desk. I gave her an update.

'Rich wants to meet up tonight,' I said, and paused. 'If I say I can't go will it put him off forever? It's just, like, I don't think I can cope with worrying about two boys and this story all at the same time.'

'Does he know about Ben?'

'I know Nita and Jake have told him something.'

'Well, then, if he has any sense and he likes you enough he'll give you time to get that sorted out in your head first.'

'You think?'

'I can't guarantee it, but hopefully – especially if he's got friends of yours trying to ease the way for you both. Unless you really don't want to see him at all, in which case you should tell all of them, now.'

I told Rich I couldn't go out but maybe another time if he wanted to. He seemed to take it OK, and Nita said she'd make sure Rich really was all right about it when she saw Jake that evening.

Anyway, I had something I needed to do. Something I wanted to check before I had my big confrontation with Dad.

Mum had been calling on a daily basis. She seemed relieved I'd survived a weekend on my own in London without being mugged or shot or enslaved in the sex trade. Of course, she didn't know what I *had* been doing – or the damage and hurt I was suffering for it now.

Strangely, I was beginning to feel pangs for boring Bath. I loved Nita to bits but I was missing Sally, and every time I called she was just about to go to this or visit that or stay somewhere else with Steve. Perhaps if I was back in Bath I could have a decent conversation with her.

I looked at my dad's old computer, sitting on his desk – the one I used to write my blog.

I pressed the 'On' button and waited as it flickered through the start-up screens.

Dad only got his new laptop a few months ago and he kept this one as a back-up. All his old files were on here; password-protected, but I had some ideas about what that password might be.

His user screen came up: Tom Dunford.

My pulse was racing; I felt uncomfortable. I'd never hacked into any of Dad's work stuff before. What I was about to do felt sneaky. I was sneaking on my father.

But then I was saved by the phone. I jumped when it rang.

It was Dad. It was almost as if he knew what I was about to do.

He said he was coming up to London and wanted to check I was OK. Could I make sure I was going to be in tomorrow evening; he was meeting someone earlier but he'd be back at the flat about eight. We could have a curry together, or anything I liked.

'We need to talk, Becky. About this story you've been working on.'

'Yeah, Dad. I need to talk to you about it too.'

After the call I closed the computer. I'd wait to speak to Dad. That's what I'd do. And then he'd tell me everything.

My stomach lurched. I still wasn't sure I wanted to hear everything.

My blog entry for Wednesday 6 August:

```
the business ed has been asking around his
contacts to see how far up this story
goes. does a minister know? does the PM
know? that wud be amazing (n awful too) if
the PM knew about it. everyone will deny
everything he says but anyway he's not
```

216

getting any further than frank reade at the moment. that either means that no one else does know or they do but have decided mr weasel is going to be the fall guy n take all the blame if (when!!) this story comes out.

james h is out on bail but has refused to speak to anyone. maybe i shud try to call cos he has nothing to lose now so he might as well tell me everything he knows. n he might feel a bit more sorry for a 17 yr old grrrl than an old hack or even a younger one like ben.

ben has still not been answering calls. i saw him over the other side of the canteen today and he did smile but then he was leaving – with sarah. n then he was outta the door. i didn't run after him cos that wud be so sad.

i am trying to make myself only think about rich.

On Wednesday afternoon Ben finally came to talk to me. He came right up to the *Sunday Style* offices and stood by my desk with his hands in his pockets. Nita's eyes widened.

'Shall we go for a coffee?' he suggested.

Claire was off sick so there was no one I needed to ask. The room was especially like a ghost-office today.

We didn't go to the canteen; he took me to the Costa place where we'd met that first time. Outside it was grey and drizzling, so we stayed under glass at a tiny circular table. I had a latte, which had become my usual.

I felt so much older than when I'd first arrived in this building; so much older even than when we were here before. I felt bruised and wise compared with the girl I was then. I kind of missed her, but I also had even more of an appetite for the world.

Ben apologised about not being in touch. He said he'd been busy, partly on another story and also on ours. (Ours? It didn't seem much like ours any more. It was days since we'd talked about it and I'd been going my own way.)

'Why haven't you been talking to me about anything?' I asked. 'Even if you don't want to talk about us that's no excuse to drop the story and not let me know what you're doing.'

'I know,' said Ben. 'I should have.' But he didn't show any sign of remorse; it was as though that was just the way it was with him and he couldn't do anything about it. Suddenly I felt as though I was the one being grown-up and he was the child.

'So why did you decide to talk to me now?'

'I didn't want . . . I don't want us to be not speaking to each other. I'd like to be friends, make up . . .'

'Friends? Not going out?'

'No, no. Like I said, I'd be no good for you. I do really admire you, and I love the way you're your own person, not trying to be anyone else. And you've got a great brain . . .' (Geez, thanks.) '. . . But I can't give you what you need.'

'And how do you know what I need?' I could feel little tweaks of anger. How dare he decide what it was I wanted or needed.

'Please, don't get upset. I'm telling you I'm rubbish. Alison told me that you know about me and her – and she gave me a really hard time about how badly I've been treating you too. So that just goes to show, doesn't it? That I'm useless with women. So you're much better off with me as a friend, not a boyfriend. It worked when we were like that – friends, and chasing this story together.'

'But you were the one who made it into something else . . .'

'I know, I know. And I know it was wrong for all kinds of reasons.' He paused. 'Though we both wanted that at the time, didn't we? I didn't force you or anything, did I?' He sounded as though he genuinely wanted reassurance that I hadn't done anything against my wishes.

'No you didn't. And you don't have to worry, I'm not going to start jumping up and down and making complaints or accusations or anything. I'm not a bunny-boiler.'

A part of me was beginning to let go of the idea of me and Ben as a couple. I felt my face relax. Perhaps we really could be friends, like Ben was saying.

He smiled. 'Don't be upset, please. I do care about you.' Ben had his hands cupped around his coffee, cradling it.

'I don't know. Perhaps we should just see if we can finish this story and get it in the paper.'

'That sounds like a good plan . . .' said Ben. 'So what have you found, then?'

I think we were both relieved to be talking about something else. It was tiring, all this emotional trauma – and complicated.

'. . . So my dad's coming this evening and I've decided I'm going to ask him about everything. He's the key. I'm sure he'll help us when he realises how important it is.'

'But, Becky – and I mean, excuse me for saying this about your dad – but what if he's involved? If he gets to that computer he could erase everything that's evidence . . .'

'Yeah, but he's not involved, I'm sure now.' Except that I wasn't. Not really. It was what I wanted to believe. Sometimes I condemned him as guilty; sometimes I thought he was innocent.

'We have to get to that computer before he does . . .' Ben wasn't listening to me.

'But he'll be back this evening and then I can ask him—'

'What time?' Ben drained the last of his coffee, suddenly filled with purpose.

'Ben . . . Why. . .?'

'You said you've got nothing you have to do this afternoon. I've got nothing I need to do either. So we go to the flat, check out the files, and then you'll have any ammunition you need before you speak to him. I'll stay while you talk to him. We can do it together . . . Remember to bring your dictaphone.'

'What? Hack into his computer now?'

'That's what I said . . .'

24

I wasn't quite sure how Ben had convinced me this was a good idea.

Here I was, sitting in front of Dad's computer again. I guessed we'd have three tries. I knew some of Dad's other passwords and they all followed the same theme – family names, and sometimes birthdays. All the kinds of things you're told not to use because they're so easy to crack. Surely for something as confidential as his work Dad would have listened to the House of Commons IT person and chosen something more cryptic. But right now I hoped he hadn't.

When had he got this computer? I thought it was when I was fourteen. I had to think back to what passwords he was using then, assuming he hadn't changed it since. (Knowing Dad he wouldn't have.)

I tried a couple of options, but they were refused. One last go.

I thought and decided and held my fingers over the keyboard, then drew back with a sigh. 'What if I get it wrong?'

'But you won't, and if you do at least we've tried. We could always take it to our IT guys at the paper and make up some story so they'd work out a way in.'

Could you do that? I wasn't sure; perhaps Ben was making it up to take the pressure off me.

So I typed in my last attempt: becky14. Dad would have been pleased with himself for using an age, not just a birth date.

It worked.

So now we had access to all of Dad's files. It took a while to work out where we might need to look.

'What's that one? "Miscellaneous"?' Ben asked, once we'd scrolled through constituency business and draft speeches and letters saying thank you but no I'm afraid I can't come to open your karaoke superstore on that day as I'll be visiting a children's hospital ward.

But Miscellaneous turned out to be stuff to do with our house – things like insurance and a letter requesting the council to do something about a tree that might cause subsidence.

'We should check the email,' I said. 'We can do a search. Look for anything with Frank Reade or James Hepworth or Auricle.'

I launched Dad's email and keyed 'Frank Reade' into the search box.

But then, just as the program was listing all the emails with Mr Weasel's name in them, I heard the sound of a key in the front door.

Terrified, I stared at Ben.

'It's him!'

'Don't worry, you carry on and look through those emails. I'll make something up and keep him away from here.' We were in Dad's study; we could close the door and shut Dad out, for a while at least, until he realised I was in here.

'But you don't understand. It's Dad's computer! He'll find me with his computer, looking at his files!'

Ben gave me an 'And what's the problem with that?' look.

And then I saw the email heading. It said 'Auricle'. Ben saw it too.

'Forward it to me, quick,' he said. 'And anything else in that thread.' My hands were shaky and sweating so that they slid on the keys. But I sent the emails to Ben – and myself, and Alison. And then I heard Alison's voice in my head asking me if it was really wise to trust Ben again.

I closed down the email program and logged out of Dad's username and back into mine.

'Hi, Dad,' I called as I went out to fill a glass of water from the kitchen tap. Much better that he knew I was here than skulking about and pretending I wasn't. But I tried to hide my face, in case my expression gave away that I wasn't feeling as breezy as I sounded.

'Becky! Hi, love. What are you doing here?' said Dad as he squeezed through the door with his holdall. 'Aren't you supposed to be at the newspaper?' And then he saw Ben in the hall. 'Oh hello. And you are . . .?'

'Ben Hutchison. I'm a friend – work colleague – of your daughter's.' He held out his hand but Dad didn't shake it.

Instead he put his holdall down on the floor and his hands on his hips.

'Ben Hutchison. I've heard a lot about you. So do you mind me asking what you're doing here with my daughter in the middle of the afternoon?' He gave Ben a stern, searching look.

'We're working on a story, Dad,' I said quietly, feeling exposed and on the verge of confessing everything we'd just been doing.

Dad glanced towards the attic stairs and my bedroom. 'So nothing's going on that I ought to know about?'

'Nothing at all,' said Ben. 'We've just been . . . working.'

'I see,' said Dad. 'Becky, is that true?' I nodded. 'Well in that case don't let me stop you . . .'

Dad had one of those Dad looks, the kind that says: 'I know you're up to something and I'm just waiting for you to give yourself away.' Ben glanced at me, then came to sit down in the living-room area, which had the kitchen-diner at one side. I stayed hanging around by the sink.

'You're here early,' I said as Dad walked over, trying not to sound as edgy as I was.

'I thought I'd drop off my bag here before my meeting – that OK with you, Becky?'

Dad was not sounding best pleased with me. I hate it when he's like that.

'Yeah, fine, whatever,' I said.

He took some files out of his bag, and his new laptop, and went through to his study. I knew I had to do it now.

'Dad . . .' I started.

'Yes, Becky?'

'You know you wanted to talk about the story I've been working on, the dirty gold one . . .'

'The one I asked you to leave alone – that one? Yes, I know.'

'Well, um, can we talk about it now?'

'I'm supposed to be somewhere in half an hour, can it wait till later?'

Then he looked at where his old computer was switched on, sitting on his desk. I flushed completely beetroot crimson postbox poppy scarlet red. I think he noticed.

'I didn't mean . . . I mean, I did . . . I wanted . . . I had to know. You know, if you were involved or not, which of course you're not, but Ben thought . . .'

'Ben thought . . .' repeated Dad.

'And I did too. That we might find out something that would really clinch the story. If we looked to see if there were any files or emails about it on your computer . . .'

It sounded pathetic. We'd been cyber-trespassing. We'd got nearly-caught, and now I was burbling stupidly, confessing everything because I felt so guilty. (This was my dad, after all. I mean, my dad – my brilliant MP dad. Of course I felt guilty.)

'Let me make a phone call, then we'll talk.' Dad appeared weary; resigned. 'Close the door will you, and could you ask your Ben friend if he can leave us alone, OK? I don't really want anyone who's not family hearing what I'm going to tell you.'

* * *

'What's going on?' asked Ben in a hushed voice.

'He's going to tell me all about it. Everything, I think,' I replied.

'But he's in there with the computer . . .'

I gave Ben a killing look. 'He's not going to do anything with the computer. Dad's not devious like that – not how your brain works!' I biffed him playfully on the head, forgetting for a moment that he wasn't Matt, or my boyfriend.

'He's asked if you can leave so he can talk to me alone,' I added. 'I think you probably should. I don't want trouble between you and Dad – or not any more than there is already.'

Ben picked up his stuff. 'If you'll be OK,' he said. 'Promise you'll call if you need me.'

He held me and I could feel his chest through his shirt, and the grip of his arms around me. He kissed my cheek; like that very first ever kiss. A friend-kiss, not a lover-kiss. But then he held on that little bit too long – that touch longer than a just-friend would.

By the time Dad came out of his study I'd made us tea. It seemed like the right thing to do. Whenever he's stressed Dad likes a cuppa.

'Thanks, sweetheart,' he said as he sat on the sofa beside me. He took a big slurp.

'So . . .' I began.

'I'll start, shall I?' said Dad. 'Because I think I need to

227

tell you a few of the things I've been keeping from you.' He sounded anxious to get everything out in the open, but also more apprehensive than I was used to. 'First of all, you do believe me, don't you, when I say I knew nothing about what Frank Reade's been up to with this Auricle business?'

'But your e—' I began, remembering the search list.

'I do know Frank,' Dad interrupted. 'I've had dealings with him. He's never been my favourite person but sometimes in government you have to do business with people you can't stand on a personal level. And there probably are some emails about Auricle, because Frank was giving evidence to our committee about mining pollution and government contracts.'

'Uhuh,' I said, deciding I'd just let Dad talk. He took another swig of tea and looked up into the air, as though arranging his thoughts on an invisible page.

'When you first told me about the dirty gold story,' he began, 'I wasn't sure what to make of it – because in committee Frank had given us a very different picture of the company, holding them up as an example of good practice and, really, now I look back on it, acting like a lobbyist for them, championing their interests. Anyway, I decided to have a chat with your editor – the editor of the paper, that is. And he said he'd been warned off. He more or less said he'd been told that if he printed, it would mean being blacklisted for all the kinds of government leaks and tip-offs that help a paper sell copies, and being refused interviews, etcetera etcetera.

'So then I knew it was serious.'

Dad paused again. For some more tea.

'I decided to look into it all myself – discreetly of course. I spoke to James Hepworth later on Friday, and when he realised who I was he revealed as much as he'd told you.'

'But I didn't tell you James's name . . .' I said.

'No, I managed to prise that out of Stephen – the editor. He's a father himself, he understood I was worried about what you might be getting into.

'And after I spoke to Mr Hepworth, that's when it started to get nasty, and personal. I'd obviously not been as discreet as I thought, because Frank Reade called me that afternoon and seemed to know about everyone I'd been talking to. In fact, my conversation with James may have been what put Frank on to knowing for sure that he was more involved in blowing the whistle on Auricle than just letting something slip by accident on a train.' Dad frowned and screwed up his face, rubbing the patch between his eyebrows as though he had a headache. 'And this is the part where I need to tell you about some things, because they're going to come out anyway. You're probably going to read some pretty unpleasant stuff about me in the papers – if we decide to go to the press and the minister with all of this.'

I gripped my teacup more tightly.

'The thing is, Becky – how am I going to tell you this . . .? Your mum and I have been keeping this from you for your own good, you understand, we didn't want you to worry.'

'About what, Dad?' I was getting seriously scared here. 'You've not got cancer or anything have you?'

'No, no, no, nothing like that. Jesus, no. Thankfully. It's nothing life-threatening, but it has been, ah, difficult, especially for your mother, I think. No, what it is . . . I've got a gambling problem. Addiction. A gambling addiction. And, um, Frank Reade told me, in no uncertain terms, that if this story got out, and I had anything to do with that happening – or you did – then he'd make it his business to guarantee the press got to hear about my problem, and he'd start a whispering campaign in the government, and in my constituency, until I'd have no career in politics worth having, and probably be forced to resign in disgrace. And he'd make sure the allegations about him were swept under the carpet and forgotten about.'

I was in shock. It was too much to take in all at once. Dad – with a gambling problem. Dad – disgraced. Frank Reade – even more of a bastard than I knew already. I remembered the shivers and bad feelings I'd got from Mr Weasel. They'd certainly been justified.

'Gambling . . . ?' I started. 'But how did that . . . Why?' I suddenly remembered the online poker sites on the computer.

Dad said that he'd explain more once we got home, that weekend, and Mum could tell it from her side too. He said that I should be kinder to Mum; that she'd had a tough time, worrying about him and money and trying to keep that strain from me – that was why she was working so hard. And

Dad was going to Gamblers Anonymous meetings, to sort himself out.

It had all started, he said, when he'd been demoted – he'd had less to do and more time on his hands, and he was depressed, he realised now. So he started playing poker with a ring that one of the South-west MPs introduced him to. It ended up taking all of his evenings, and he and Mum had needed to remortgage our house because of the money he'd lost.

'There are people where it's much worse, though. Families where it pulls their whole lives apart,' Dad continued. 'I know in a way I've had a lucky escape, because your mother has made me confront it in time.'

'What about those online poker sites? Are you still gambling?' I asked, in a tone of voice that sounded shockingly like my mother's.

'Sometimes, I have to admit. I haven't completely cracked it yet but it's much more . . . under control.'

'So this is what you meant when you said there were things it was better I didn't know?'

'Partly, yes.'

I went over to Dad and gave him a big hug. I felt tears pushing their way into my eyes. Dad looked as though he was about to cry too.

'I'm sorry I ever even thought for a second you might be involved with Auricle.'

'And I'm sorry that I've let you down, Becky.'

In the past, I would've said that anyone with a gambling

problem was stupid and had no self-control. But if it had happened to my dad . . . Well, I had to think again about that one.

But there were still some things I needed to know, so I could fit everything together in my mind. 'So what were you doing at that party, the one at Wembley?'

'I went there to meet Frank Reade and tell him that he didn't need to worry, because I'd decided I wasn't going to take things any further. But that he'd better not do anything or leak anything, and he should lay off James too, or I might change my ideas. I also told him I'd make sure you dropped the story.'

'But Dad . . .'

'I know, it sounds spineless, and I know I shouldn't have spoken for you like that . . . But I just wanted him to leave us all alone. I was so angry, but I didn't know what else to do right then.'

Everything was still whirring in my head.

'So why didn't you drag me away from the party?' (That's what Mum would have done.)

'The truth is I didn't recognise you at first – you looked stunning, by the way.'

Dad smiled a crinkle-eyed smile at me for the first time since he'd come in, and I couldn't help myself grinning back.

'Then I was going to come over and give you a talking to for completely ignoring what I'd said on the phone,' he continued, 'but I didn't want to draw Frank's attention to you. And then later, after his slimy assurances that everything was going to be hunky-dory, I didn't want to alarm you. I thought I could handle it. Why shouldn't you have your weekend in London? And you'd be leaving the paper soon anyway. I thought you wouldn't make the connection to Frank in that time, so I wouldn't have to lay a three-line whip on you to stop – but it seems I underestimated my daughter.'

Dad lifted his cup to drink, but the tea was finished.

'To be honest, I was wrestling with myself, too – deciding what to do for the best. Then I saw about James, and heard you were well on the way to clinching the story. So I couldn't hide from it any more – I knew I needed to tell you everything.'

'And what do we do now?' I asked.

'What do you think we should do, Becky?'

25

The next day I strode into the office feeling shellshocked but certain. I knew what I was going to do. All I needed was to finish piecing everything together, put in the quotes from Dad that we'd agreed, and present it to the *Courier*'s editor. Dad had made an appointment with him, to come in and back me up. Alison was primed for any help I wanted with the writing. But I'd heard nothing from Ben.

I took the lift to his floor and went to Ben's desk. 'Hi, Sarah – where's Ben?'

'Think he's gone to get something to eat,' she said, still typing as she spoke.

'OK. Thanks.'

I looked at Ben's screen, and saw the word 'Auricle' up at the top of a document he had open. I started to read it. And then I sat down to read more.

I couldn't believe it – Ben had written up our story (my story!) without talking to me about it, and using the emails from my dad's computer. (In the emails Frank Reade had said he could personally vouch for Auricle being an upstanding company, and the Environmental Audit

Committee should treat them as a trusted source!)

Anger started to rise in me. How dare Ben go ahead like this, with something that involved not only me but my dad too! Why hadn't he told me?

What I saw next was the final straw. At the top of the article he'd typed: 'By Ben Hutchison' – no mention of my name, until you got to the end, and then it said: 'With additional reporting by Becky Dunford'.

'Oh . . .' said a man's voice behind me.

I turned around to see Ben standing with a croissant in one hand and a coffee in the other. He'd taken a bite from the croissant and there were flakes of pastry around his mouth.

I folded my arms. 'Can you explain this, please, Ben?'

'I've written up the article – I was just about to bring it up to show you.'

Yeah, right. Like I'd believe that one.

'So why didn't you ask me about my conversation with my dad? About what he actually said rather than what you've made up here about what he supposedly said to you?'

'That's just a first draft, Becky. Like I said, I was going to come and talk to you about it all, and add in what your father told you. I just wanted to get ahead with it so I could take it in to Stephen nice and early and it could run in tomorrow's paper. It could be front-page news – that's what you wanted, isn't it, Becky?'

Then he realised that everyone around us had gone quiet and was listening. Journalists had stopped typing; people had quickly finished phone calls so they could hear better what we were saying.

'Let's go and talk about this somewhere else,' said Ben. He dumped his croissant and his drink down on the desk. Some of the coffee slopped over on to his hand. 'Ouch,' he muttered, and wiped it on his trousers.

We went out into the stairwell. It wasn't completely private, but better than a roomful of journalists.

'Becky, look, you have to believe me that I wasn't going to just go ahead with the story without talking to you at all.'

'But you weren't going to put my name at the top of it, were you? I wouldn't mind if your name had come first in a joint byline – "By Ben Hutchison and Becky Dunford" – but all you'd written was a measly "Additional reporting by . . ." at the bottom.'

'Well, I am the one who's a professional journalist . . .'

That sounded so patronising and pompous.

'I can't believe you just said that! It's like you're seeing me as a kid. So I'm a grown-up when you want to sleep with me but not adult enough to be treated as an equal when it comes to a newspaper story . . .'

Ouch. I could see I'd hit home. Ben looked genuinely shocked, as though he hadn't realised until then what he'd been doing.

'Becky, that sounds awful. Please don't think that of me. I do respect you. Really. Whatever you may think.'

Perhaps he was telling the truth. But even if he was, the way he'd treated me since the Wembley evening had been shabby.

'Look, Ben, I don't know if you're being honest with me now or not. But why should I believe you after the way you've behaved with me? I know you warned me about your being fucked up – but then you just went straight ahead and did what you wanted anyway. If you're supposed to be the one who's older and wiser and more professional, how do you explain that?'

'I'm sorry, Becky. I've been useless, haven't I? I really only want the best for you.'

'But can you understand, Ben – that's not how it looks from my side. It may be how you justify it in your head, but the way you've acted with me doesn't feel like it's been in my best interests at all. You really do have some serious sorting out – and growing up – to do.'

Ben kept his head down, looking at his feet.

'Look, my dad's got an appointment with the editor this afternoon to talk about Auricle. I'm not going to be petty and say it's only my story – because I know I wouldn't have been able to write it without you. So I think the fairest thing is a joint byline.'

'OK.'

'But I'd like to write the article my way.'

'OK.'

Ben looked defeated.

Could we really ever be friends, after all this? It seemed so sad – we'd got on so well as a team, and now that closeness was most probably all going to be lost. But at least

I'd had my say. I hadn't been a doormat. Sally would be so proud of me. And Alison and Nita.

My blog entry for Tuesday 12 August:

everything has bin moving too fast for me to have time to catch u up here on all of it as it happens. if u have not seen the articles in the *courier* then this is the quick version . . .

after the first front-page story appeared james h decided to come clean n give his whole statement to me (well dad but i was there too with my trusty dictaphone) and dad took that to some high-ups in the govt n has demanded an inquiry. but we don't know what will happen yet. dad thinks it will be enough to mean auricle has at the very least to make a grovelling public apology n heads will roll there - n almost certainly mr weasel's too. the police are investigating to see if there's a fraud case n looking into what frank r did to james - perverting the course of justice or something by fitting him up.

dad has arranged for the *courier's* editor

– who he has got to know quite well now – to do an interview with him where he is going to admit to everyone that he has a gambling problem n offer to resign if he doesn't get the support of his constituency. (here is a link to gamblers anonymous if you or your family also have a problem like this.)

he said that if he has to stop being an mp after all of this then he will go back to teaching at the uni if they'll have him. i have bin trying to be nicer to mum. we had a big heart 2 heart and made up. there's still something matt swears he overheard her say once about me that i haven't confronted her with yet but i feel maybe one day i will now.

on our last day at *sunday style* there was a bit of a party for me n nita – if some cake n fruit juice is what you call a party. it was more like we were six yrs old!! but it was sweet of them. what was fantastic was the design dept had made us both covers of the mag (fake ones not real) with pix of us on them. nita's said stuff like 'nita mistry: stylist to the stars' with her looking perfect as usual, n mine had me trekking with a backpack from one of our holidays n said 'our campaigning reporter aims to turn the world green' n also 'celebs lock up your secrets – no wrongdoing is safe with becky dunford on your trail!'

but the most incredible, wonderful thing is that the bbc has rung to ask me n dad to go on *newsnight* together! can u believe that? this is my dream come true!!!

26

The grass was going brown and the earth was baked hard and cracking. It was up to the thirties Celsius and all around the country there were record temperatures. The ground at the V festival was littered with trodden-in food and empty drinks bottles. As fast as the cleaners came around to clear them up, the debris reappeared.

Girls were wearing bikinis, and not much else, and boys were in shorts, throwing whatever water they could find over themselves and each other. A pong rippled out from the ladies toilet block as I waited in the queue. In the background I could hear familiar tunes coming from the main stage. I'd wanted to see this band but the queue was inching along sooo slowly. By the time I reached the cubicles the set would be over. There were fields not far away, ideal for a sneaky pee – but they were on the other side of the fence and the security.

I gazed longingly across the colony of festival-goers, towards the tented arc of the stage. Nita and Jake would be there, and Rich and the rest of Sharpedge, who were headlining one of the smaller tents later in the evening.

Sally was off somewhere with Steve.

'I reckon,' said the girl next to me, 'that I could charm the security to let us go through and piss in that field. Whaddayou think?'

She was striking, with dark hair swept up and off her face, and rich olive skin. She had on a red bikini top and white cut-off hotpants, and big sunglasses with white frames. She was more than pretty.

'I think we might be waiting all night if we stay here,' I said. 'I'm willing to try if you are.' If it didn't work, we'd have lost our places in the queue, but I was bored and hot and fed up with hanging around here. It was worth the risk.

'OK. Shall we go?'

The girl sauntered over with a sexy sway in her hips, as though she was on a runway, or walking up a premiere red carpet. She stood up close to one of the men on security and started talking and joking with him. After a few milliseconds – or so it seemed compared with the interminable loo wait – we were through the gate.

We ran to the field and found some hedge that gave us enough cover.

'Oh I needed that so bad!' the girl said when we were finished.

'Me too,' I replied. 'I'm Becky, by the way.'

'Ellie,' said the girl. 'Pleased to meet you. Do you do this often?'

'What? Festivals or pissing in fields?'

'Both,' she said.

I explained about Rich and Sharpedge as we made our way back through the gate and Ellie flashed a gorgeous smile at the security guy. She said she was in a band too, but they hadn't managed to break through – yet – not like Sharpedge. It was hard, she said, trying to make things happen if you didn't have someone with money and contacts backing you, or a PR launch like those people on shows like *Pop Idol* or *Fame Academy*. But she seemed pretty convinced it was only a matter of 'when', not 'if'.

'So what are your band like?' I asked.

'I've got a track on my iPod – d'you fancy a listen?'

Ellie handed me her headphones. 'It's great,' I said. 'I like it – especially your voice.' (And I wasn't just being polite.) 'Isn't there anything else you can do to get yourselves some attention?'

'Well, I don't know if I should tell you . . .' Ellie was beaming, as though she was pleased with herself, but looking shifty at the same time, scuffing her trainers in the dirt and turning her head to look around behind her. 'Swear if you ever meet any of my band you won't breathe a word of this, OK?'

'OK,' I said, intrigued.

'The thing is, I've already auditioned for one of those talent shows – *Pop World*. I'm just waiting to hear if I've got to the next stage. You don't think that's terrible, do you? I mean, I did it without the rest of the band knowing. But it just feels like it's up to me to give things a push. And I want to make it so much. I just can't think about it not happening . . .'

Personally, I wasn't sure about going behind your friends' backs – I wasn't too keen at the moment on people not being entirely open. But I didn't know the full story, so it wouldn't be fair to leap in and judge. And anyway, on first meeting I liked Ellie – my instinct was that I wanted to help her if I could (and return the toilet queue favour). *Pop World* rang a bell – and then I remembered . . .

'I don't know if it'll help, but when I was doing some research for an article about *Supermodel School* I spoke to someone at the production company who said she was working on *Pop World* too.'

'Oh, really?' said Ellie, sounding interested.

'It might not be any use, but why don't you give me your email address anyway, and I'll see if she's got any inside information.'

'That would be fantastic,' said Ellie. 'Thanks.'

I found a pen in my bag (well, I was a proper journalist now, so I needed to make sure I could take notes anywhere I went) and wrote my email on Ellie's hand, and scribbled hers in my even-more-dogeared-than-usual notebook.

To my surprise, Ellie gave me a big kiss on the cheek. 'I'd better go find my mates now, OK? Catch you later.'

She scooted off and I called Nita to find out where they were among all these bodies. I navigated my way, in constant telephone contact, stepping over outstretched legs and empty cans, and then pushing past sweaty, dancing, chanting bodies.

Rich gave me a kiss when I reached him. 'You've been ages, babe. I thought you'd got lost. And Manny here realised after you'd gone, you could've taken my pass and got yourself into the VIP area.'

'Never mind,' I said, 'I'm here now.'

Rich squinted at my face. 'What's that? Looks like lipstick.'

'Oh, I met this girl in the toilet queue and we got chatting,' I said, rubbing at where I thought the mark was.

Then the crowd erupted into roars and clapping.

I felt my phone buzz in my hand. It was Matt.

'What?' I shouted. 'I can't hear, it's too loud here. I'm at a festival remember . . . Fest-i-val. What . . . ? No, I've got my volume up full, I can't make it any louder . . . Say that again . . . Really . . . ? No . . . ! That's incredible! I'm so pleased. I'm so happy for Dad. Tell him I'll call later, when it's quieter. Bye. See you. Bye, Matt.'

I closed the phone.

'Frank Reade's resigned,' I announced, with the biggest smile on my face. 'And the police say they're looking into bringing charges. It sounds like he'd been getting kickbacks from Auricle, in return for not letting out about their dirty gold and lobbying the government on their behalf.'

'Frank?' said Rich.

'You know, the bastard who's caused so much trouble, the one I've been doing those stories about.'

'Yeah, of course. That's great, babe,' said Rich as he rocked along with the music, mouthing the words.

Nita came and gave me a big hug. 'I knew you'd get him,' she whispered in my ear.

By the time Sharpedge were due to come on the sun had set and the last blue light was fading from the horizon. The evening was what you'd call sultry. Stars dotted the clear sky high above the auras of the stage lights.

Nita and I cheered ourselves hoarse as Sharpedge played. I think I spotted Ellie over the other side of the tent.

My boyfriend was wowing the crowds up on stage and I'd helped to bring a man I loathed to justice. Music, night-time, friends, dancing – all these things combined into a flying adrenaline high. And then, in the middle of the joy, a shaft of sadness sliced through me. Only a moment. A pang about Ben and a second of wondering what might have been if he'd behaved differently; a moment of thinking about my dad and the gambling; and about the way things had been so scratchy the past years between me and my mum.

And then it faded. And the being here now took over again.

Turn over to read the

consequence

of this story...

Prologue

I was trying to dance, but my left foot was trapped underneath a bit of railing at the front of the crowd. I must have looked like a dislocated frog or something, all right side and no rhythm. It wasn't the image I'd been aiming for, but I tried to appear cool and in control as Andy grinned a toothy grin at me and I felt the growing excitement in the sounds that swirled around us.

'God I love you, Ellie!' he shouted, actually aiming it at the sky not me. It sounded something like 'Grod a luff bug hell' by the time it got to me, because the music was pounding between us and the lights obscured his mouth. It didn't really matter, because we'd finally made it to the V festival, together with all our mates: Dylan, Jamie, Kate – and it was the best Saturday night there'd ever been, ever.

I looked behind me, doing little one-legged jumps up and down, trying to see to the back of the crowd in the insane dancing of the strobe lights, trying to get a grip on the scale of it.

Yeah, like that was ever going to happen: there were so many people moving just like me that I couldn't even see beyond the group of lads right behind us with their shirts wrapped around their heads.

'I love you too, Andy . . .' I screamed, throwing my arms around his neck and being pulled towards him, his strength finally freeing me from my temporary little prison.

I looked up at the huge stage in front of me in wonder. The Last Kiss were on fire tonight. They were tearing through their first single as if there was no tomorrow, and for all I cared, there wouldn't be. This was as perfect as it got.

I grinned at Dylan to my left: he was buzzing on the dope he'd scored earlier in the day when we first arrived. I pulled him down into the bear hug that Andy and I had been sharing and nuzzled both their sweaty heads into my own, suddenly getting lifted off the ground by them in the process.

'I love both of you,' I screeched. 'And it'll be me up there next year! And you,' I shouted, just as they started to push me further up towards their shoulders, laughing together at how easy it was to lift me. 'Don't drop me, whatever you do . . .' I screamed.

I was a bit worried about breaking my neck, but I knew the TV cameras always focused in on girls who were up on guys' shoulders in the crowd. How tragic would it be to get dropped just at that perfect moment when they focused in on my face for the sing-along chorus at the end?

I looked back down and saw my best friends all around me, my band. I took in the crowd at last, finally getting a sense of proportion. We were caught up in a swaying lump of humanity as far as the eye could see.

I turned to the stage and grinned like a mad woman and realised that I just couldn't imagine a world without music, without my friends, my band and my dreams.

Nothing before or since had ever made me think it wasn't going to happen for me. And this was just the confirmation. I raised my arms above my head and started to move to the music.

All this really was going to be mine one day, if I wanted it.

And trust me, I did.